"Angel, do you believe in love at first sight?" David asked, his lips only a breath away from hers.

"Yes." She said it unequivocally.

"I don't." He held her away from him then. "Much as I'd like to, I just can't lie to you about this." He kissed the tip of her nose and called himself seven kinds of a fool. How could any guy in his right mind turn down the chance to make love to a genuine angel? "I have doubts I'd be any good for you. I'm too . . ." Too scared to admit she was the best thing to happen to him, too scared of loving and losing to risk loving again?

"You're too pessimistic," Angela said brightly. "But take heart. I specialize in miracles, and I've got all night to work on you."

"Don't you ever take no for an answer?" David asked.

"Oh, once when I was six. But not tonight," she murmured lovingly.

"Do you realize how much trouble we could get into if anybody finds us together like this?" he asked.

"No more trouble than if nobody finds us."

He groaned. Resistance was useless. . . .

WHAT ARE *LOVESWEPT* ROMANCES?

They are stories of true romance and touching emotion. We believe those two very important ingredients are constants in our highly sensual and very believable stories in the *LOVESWEPT* line. Our goal is to give you, the reader, stories of consistently high quality that may sometimes make you laugh, sometimes make you cry, but are always fresh and creative and contain many delightful surprises within their pages.

Most romance fans read an enormous number of books. Those they truly love, they keep. Others may be traded with friends and soon forgotten. We hope that each *LOVESWEPT* romance will be a treasure—a "keeper." We will always try to publish

LOVE STORIES YOU'LL NEVER FORGET
BY AUTHORS YOU'LL ALWAYS REMEMBER

The Editors

LOVESWEPT® • 212

Margie McDonnell
Banish the Dragons

BANTAM BOOKS
TORONTO · NEW YORK · LONDON · SYDNEY · AUCKLAND

BANISH THE DRAGONS

A Bantam Book / October 1987

*LOVESWEPT® and the wave device are registered
trademarks of Bantam Books, Inc. Registered in U.S. Patent
and Trademark Office and elsewhere.*

*If you would be interested in receiving protective vinyl
covers for your Loveswept books, please write to this address
for information:*

*Loveswept
Bantam Books
P.O. Box 985
Hicksville, NY 11802*

ISBN 0-553-21843-3

Published simultaneously in the United States and Canada

---

*Bantam Books are published by Bantam Books, Inc. Its trade-
mark, consisting of the words "Bantam Books" and the por-
trayal of a rooster, is Registered in U.S. Patent and Trademark
Office and in other countries. Marca Registrada. Bantam
Books, Inc., 666 Fifth Avenue, New York, New York 10103.*

PRINTED IN THE UNITED STATES OF AMERICA

O   0 9 8 7 6 5 4 3 2 1

In Memory of
Dad & Grandpa
and
For The One True Knight of Steel
With the power to Banish The Dragons

One

It was monstrously large, huge enough to devour anything and anyone in its path, and it was getting bigger all the time. It was ugly, even for a dragon; its slime-covered scales were a mottled gray-green like the color of mold on old bread or the muck on the bottom of a swamp. It reeked of brimstone and decay and the stench of death. Only its eyes glowed alive and red and voraciously hungry. Mindless and terrifying, it stalked and killed at random. Always before, though, chance had taken it elsewhere. Now it had seized the little princess, made her its captive, and before long it would destroy her. . . .

Angela Newman snapped the portable tape recorder off. It was useless. She wasn't going to get any work done while she waited in this empty, simply decorated office. Those words would never do in a children's story. Nor would the pen-and-ink drawing under her fingers. She viciously crumpled the sketch of the loathsome-looking dragon, as if shredding the paper monster could somehow banish the real dragon that had inspired the ghoulish fairy tale.

"And you're supposed to create some of the best children's stories around?" she asked herself aloud, answering with a snort of self-derision. "Reading this story would give a kid terminal insomnia."

Terminal. There was that word again. She'd forbidden everyone to say it in her presence, but she couldn't always manage to keep it from her own thoughts. *Terminal.* Even the word was insidious and ugly, rather like the dragon in her nightmarish bedtime story. Janet had first used the term when she'd called to deliver the grim news. Angela vividly recalled hanging up and calling her sister back, absolutely sure that the call had been to someone else, from someone else, about someone else. *Terminal* was a word that simply *couldn't* apply to a child as precious to her as her nine-year-old niece Liz was. Up until a year ago when Janet married Army Captain Tom Lewis and moved to his duty station in Korea, Liz had seemed fine.

Only she hadn't been, not on the inside. Every doctor between Korea and the U.S. agreed on that. Liz had cancer. What Angela refused to accept was that she had *terminal* cancer. Terminal implied that hope was impossible. Angela had never believed in impossibilities. Ten years ago when a fire destroyed the family's printing business and took their parents and Janet's first husband with it, Angela had heard the word *impossible* a lot. No one believed that an eighteen-year-old girl could finish high school and college while supporting a pregnant sister and rebuilding the family business too. Impossible or not, Angela had done it anyway, until today, as president of a flourishing printing and publishing company, and one of its best authors, very few people told her anything was impossible.

She smiled in grim determination. Hope for Liz was right around the corner, if not in Korea, then in the U.S. And since Janet couldn't care for both her newborn twins *and* a critically ill child, Angela had taken over, at least for now. And everything had seemed to be okay. They'd followed all the instructions, even sending Liz to the Casa de los Niños summer camp, which was tailored to the needs of terminally ill kids. But that had been a mistake. She'd thought so in the beginning. Liz didn't belong in a camp for kids who were likely to *die*. That idea had been confirmed when Liz called this morning during an executive staff meeting. The child was sobbing so hard she couldn't even speak coherently. Angela had stormed out of the office, and driven the two hundred miles from Los Angeles to the Casa de los Niños summer camp, breaking speed limits all the way. And all she knew was that the man who was responsible, Staff Counselor David Ortega, was too busy to see her.

Angela's head jerked up sharply as Ortega's secretary emerged—alone, Angela noted—from the inner sanctum.

"I'm sorry, Ms. Newman." She shook her head in apology. "Mr. Ortega is still tied up on that phone call. I'm afraid unless you'd care to come back later, you'll just have to wait."

"Wait?" She jumped to her feet and marched across the room. "If I wait here much longer, the administrators of the camp could legitimately charge me rent! In fact, speaking of administrators—" she leaned vulturelike over the desk and pounced on one of the camp's publicity folders—"just show me where to find whoever's in charge of personnel and I won't need to see your boss." Having the blasted man fired wouldn't be as emotionally satisfying as telling him he was seven kinds of a louse to his face, but it would do. She had no intention of waiting around here all day when, somewhere out there, Liz needed her.

"Mr. Lamont is actually in charge of personnel," the young woman began. "But—"

"His office is where?" Angela cut off whatever explanations she might have given and thrust a map under her nose.

"Well, here . . ." She pointed to a place on the map. "But he's not there now. He's on vacation and so his duties fall to the administrator next in line."

It was like playing twenty questions. "Who is . . ." Angela prompted.

"Mr. Ortega."

Angela struck her balled-up fist on the desk, withdrawing it quickly with a cry of pain. A paper clip clung to the skin below her little finger.

"Ms. Newman? Ms. Newman, are you all right?"

It was a question filled with genuine concern that nevertheless made Angela feel like screaming an enraged response. All right? All right? How in God's name could she be all right when the dragon was mercilessly devouring the little princess even as they spoke, and a sadistic dungeon master was probing the wounds?

She pressed her lips together tightly, trying to remind herself that none of this was the secretary's fault. "I'll be much better, thank you, just as soon as the counselor *gets off the phone*! He's been closeted in there long enough to talk to the

President of the United States and E.T.!" Angela pulled the paper clip out of her skin and dabbed at the blood oozing from the small wound.

The secretary winced. "Maybe I'd better get you a Band-Aid."

"You do that," Angela murmured as the young woman disappeared into another room. *And take your time*, she added silently. Images of Liz flooded her mind, hardening her resolve; Liz crying while some old, rheumy-eyed, wispy-haired Sigmund Freud type discussed behavior modification techniques over the phone; Liz huddled alone and afraid while some sadistic shrink. . . .

She stood up and made for the closed office door. She hadn't spent six months fighting hostile government officials, narrow-minded physicians, hospital red tape, and hopelessness just to be bested by some stodgy clinician who couldn't care less about the trouble he'd caused! Her emerald-green eyes snapped with fury. He'd care before she got through with him. She'd make him care or she'd see him buried in trouble up to his myopic eyeballs and wispy hair! Pushing the door open, she strode into his office, her nostrils flared and as ready to breathe fire as any dragon.

Staff Counselor David Ortega used his free hand to massage the side of his aching head. He held the telephone receiver in his free hand. It was a subterfuge. The party on the other end of the line had hung up a full minute ago. If he had an ounce of true professionalism, he'd hang up, too, and let Jane admit the person in his outer office who wanted so badly to see him. Part of his job was to have an open-door policy. Just at the moment, though, he didn't want the damn door open, and he'd lost the last shred of his professionalism along with what little patience and optimism he still possessed.

It had been a difficult day. Not only was he supposed to take care of his regular duties, he'd neglected to do his daily reports for a week and was thus forced to do them all marathon-style today or explain why he hadn't done them to the program director. On top of that, Bob Lamont's responsibilities, such as they were, had fallen to him. So in addition to conducting an orientation class for the new campers, holding a round-table discussion on death and dying, he'd also had to decide whether to fire one groundskeeper or hire one cook's helper. Or was it the other way around? No matter. He'd put everything on hold anyway as soon as the expected telephone call from Scott's parents came through.

Scott hadn't been at the camp long, less than a week in fact, but he'd struck a responsive chord in David's heart, and it had hurt like hell when it had become necessary to fly Scott to the nearest hospital. It had only been a matter of time. David knew that. Everybody had known that. But a numbing cold had settled over him after he'd gotten that phone call, and he just wasn't up to putting on a professional, impersonal act for the person who was annoying his secretary. Tomorrow. He'd see whoever it was tomorrow. Or better yet, refer whoever it was to his female counterpart at the camp, Sylvia Krisik. Sylvia still owed him for a couple of times when he'd covered for her. He pushed a button on his telephone and waited for his secretary Jane to respond. Maybe this was what job burnout felt like. He'd have to remember to reread the article on it in last month's medical journal. In his position he couldn't afford to hope for miracles that were impossible, and then fall apart emotionally when they didn't come true.

"It's not quitting time yet, Jane," he muttered into the telephone. "If it was quitting time, I'd be in my cabin with a tall Scotch—" He looked up at the sound of footsteps. Jane must have read his mind. It took only a split second to realize that the whirling dervish who careened into his office was *not* Jane. Jane was efficient; even better, she was unobtrusive. She did her job quietly and without distracting him from *his* job. The woman before him now would be a major distraction if she was standing still. She wasn't standing still. After slamming the door into the wall, which resulted in knocking one picture, two diplomas, and a houseplant down, she descended on his neatly organized desk and swept a week's worth of his paperwork to the floor. She moved with the speed and grace of a lioness running prey to the ground, and she had all the subtlety of an exploding volcano.

"I don't know who you think you are, or what Cracker Jack box you got your diploma from, mister, but if you try to fold, spindle, or mutilate my niece's psyche one more time, I promise that I'll personally tear your credentials up into itty-bitty pieces and feed them to you for breakfast!"

It was one of those rare moments in his life when everything seemed to happen in slow motion. Stacks of unnumbered reports filtered slowly to the floor at her feet, and a part of his mind registered the fact that he was going to have to pick them up. Not only would he not be in his easy chair at 5:15 with a tall Scotch, he'd be lucky to be in bed before midnight tonight. Still, he was much more interested in looking at her than he was in worrying over spilt milk.

She was beautiful, although not in the traditional sense of the word, particularly not if you liked the Madonna sort of woman. Her small, oval face was contorted with determination and wrath, her flashing green eyes an even better mirror to her feelings. Her face was flushed, but he could still see a sprinkling of freckles where her complexion had been kissed by the sun. Her hair seemed an unlikely combination of blond, red, and brown, and looked as though it had been combed in a wind tunnel, the shoulder-length curls skewed at odd angles to her head. Her cream-colored suit indicated that she was some sort of a businesswoman, yet the starkly tailored clothing did nothing to hide her femininity or its sensual allure. On the tiny side, not over five feet three and not more than 105 pounds soaking wet, she was perfectly proportioned, her body slim and athletic. Her body canted toward his desk, her breasts straining at the material of her pale pink silk blouse, she placed her hands on her hips.

"Well?" she demanded impatiently. "Are you going to put that stupid thing down or has it grown to the side of your head?"

He looked at her blankly, and then, with dawning understanding, replaced the telephone receiver. Actually he should be grateful to her for the excuse. He hadn't put the phone down since Scott's parents had called. He got up from behind the desk and waded through the debris surrounding it to reach her.

"You'll have to excuse my discourtesy," he said dryly. "Usually my secretary waits until I'm off the phone before sending anybody in to see me. She must have slipped up."

"No 'up' about it! She slipped out and I slipped in. If she hadn't, I'd have been waiting out there until hell froze over." Angela marched up to his chest and stabbed him in the sternum with her forefinger. Good grief, he was tall, she thought. No matter. She fully intended to cut him down to size. "I don't have the time for small talk. My name is Angela Newman, and I'm here to see you about your unethical, not to mention cruel, treatment of my niece Liz Lewis."

Liz? David searched his memory for a face to go along with the name. He saw so many kids come through the camp, some staying only a few days. Heaven knew he did his best to get to know them all. . . . No; he did a quick rethink. He did his best to get to know their names. He tried not to get to know them too well. He'd known Scott far too well. Liz . . . Liz? Liz! Aha! The pieces fell together. Elizabeth! The little girl who'd come in a couple of days ago with terminal cancer. The little girl who'd befriended Scott at the last, and who'd been so upset to learn that her friend wasn't coming back. He should have known.

"I understand why you're here. I should have expected you." He reached out to put a comforting hand on her arm.

Angela drew back with a jerk, breaking the contact between them almost instantly. For just a moment when his hand had closed over her upper arm, she'd felt a surprising jolt of . . . of *something*, something like hot and cold and electricity all mixed together. She looked up into his face, really seeing him and not just her anger for the first time.

David rubbed his fingers, mumbled something, and reached across the desk to pick up the telephone again. He dialed the extension to one of the cabins twice before getting it right. Maybe he was growing senile? No, definitely not senile. The surge of animal attraction that had arced between him and this woman, temporarily befuddling him, certainly didn't have anything to do with senility. "Hello? Cabin B? Sarah, this is David Ortega. Would you locate Elizabeth . . . ah, Liz Lewis, please, and have her report to my office? We have a little problem that needs to be ironed out." Replacing the receiver, he rubbed his fingers again and turned back to the "little problem" he'd referred to. She was staring holes through him, and small in stature though she might be, he had a feeling she could cause him big trouble.

"You don't look like Sigmund Freud."

David shook his head at what sounded to be an accusation. "Thankfully not. He's been dead for over forty-five years."

"You're not old and you don't have wispy hair."

"I'm working on it." He scrambled to gather his shattered wits. "I'm only thirty-five. You'll have to give me a few years."

Angela scowled suspiciously. "You *are* David Ortega, the counselor here, aren't you? I mean, I haven't gone through all this to confront a janitor or something, have I?"

A janitor? "I think I'm the counselor, at least I was this morning." He searched through the daily reports which were scattered all over the floor, setting some on the desk and others on the swivel chair. Somewhere, probably on the bottom, was Elizabeth Lewis's report. Naturally he couldn't find it now when he needed it. The janitor probably could have. "Unless this is all a nightmare and I'm really someone else." Fat chance.

"Oh, no. You're not going to weasel out of this one so easily." She followed his progress through the paper-covered carpet, replacing her fantasy image with a real one. That was the trouble with a vivid imagination; you could never count on it for accuracy. Sigmund Freud and his wispy hair marched haughtily back into her creative mind along with *stodgy, old,* and *myopic.* David Ortega had nothing in common with any of them, or for that matter with any of the other psychologists Angela had met because of Liz's problems. For starters, he didn't look one bit professional. His tanned, tall body was clothed in tight, faded blue jeans, ridiculous orange tennis shoes, and a stained, ragged-edged sweatshirt that read: *Wanna play doctor? I need the practice.* Dressed as he was, he looked more like a member of one of the punk rock bands Liz was so crazy about. So all right, he wasn't stodgy. His hair wasn't wispy either. On the contrary, it was a thick, dark sable, springy and on the longish side, as if a trip to the barber was low on his list of priorities. And finally, he wasn't myopic. She was sure he could see her quite well. He had, in fact, stopped searching through his papers, and was looking at her as though she were some prized lab rat. His eyes were piercingly blue and his expressive gaze was strangely intimate.

"I'm sorry . . ." He looked around the floor as if expecting the required paper to levitate itself into his line of vision. "I can't seem to find Liz's file, but I remember some of her background, and I'm sure you can fill me in on the pertinent details before she arrives."

His voice was low and gravelly, a little like hers after a bad cold. It sounded much better coming from him. It threw her off guard, left her feeling vulnerable and strange. Still, it didn't matter what he looked like or how he made *her* feel. It was how he'd made Liz feel that mattered. And Liz had said he'd made her cry.

"The only pertinent thing you need to know is that I'm taking Liz out of here today before you can do her any further harm. Do you know that she called me this morning? She couldn't even get out an explanation because she was sobbing. All I know for sure is that *you* said something to hurt her." Her emerald-green eyes fixed frostily on him. "And I've had it with people hurting her while I'm in charge."

She was in charge of Liz? The explanation for that was surely in the report which he still hadn't found. He went back to looking. "You're responsible for Liz?" Where was that damnable report?

"Ever since she was diagnosed." Her voice betrayed a slight quiver as she relived the last several months. "My sister, Janet, had just given birth to twins and couldn't travel, let alone take on the responsibility of caring for two newborns *and* a critically ill child. That's why she entrusted Liz to me. I'm *supposed* to watch out for her. . . ." She took three or four steps toward the door in frustration, reshuffling some of David's shifting mountain of paperwork. Why was she bothering to explain herself to someone who was too busy crawling around on all fours to listen?

"I'm listening to you." Accurately reading her facial expressions he dug through the notes at a faster pace, tossing handfuls of them under his desk and behind his back. "It's just that I'm looking and listening at the same time. You see, I know I wrote down a few notes while Liz and I talked. If I can find them . . ." He pounced on a likely looking memo. Drat! It was the wrong likely looking memo. "If I find them, then you'll understand what I said and what I was trying to do."

"That's just it! I'm sick, sick, sick of being told I have to understand what you're all *trying* to do, when as far as I can see the only thing anyone's actually doing is hurting her. And don't tell me I have to give it a fair chance. I've tried!" The words tumbled out on their own, her feelings held inside too long to be contained once released. "I did all the conventional things. I know every oncologist, every cancer specialist in the state on a first-name basis. My medicine cabinet has grown to three drawers and a cupboard. I have enough chemicals in my house to be arrested for big-time drug trafficking. And it's a wonder *I* don't glow in the dark from all the radiation therapy *Liz* has had." She ran a hand through her hair, combing it straight back and out of pain-filled eyes with her fingers. "We've gone to L.A. for acupuncture, to Mexico for laetrile, to churches for group prayer, to psychic healers for mystical cures, and to some people for some things I'd really rather not remember. And, you know, through it all, I've stood back and watched them poke and prod and examine and inject that little girl without trying to stop it." Caught up in the memories, she was only vaguely aware that he had given up on his search for the papers, and was now standing in front of her, listening intently to her every word. "We followed up on everyone's advice, ridiculous or not. Somebody said cancer patients shouldn't eat meat, chemicals, or preservatives, so we rototilled the front yard and lived like rabbits on home-grown lettuce, carrots, and tomatoes." A single tear ran down her cheek.

David stopped thinking like a psychologist and started thinking like a man, pulling her into his arms in an instinctive attempt to soothe her with his touch.

"We read how humor was found to be therapeutic in some cases." She laughed bitterly and wiped her tears on his sweatshirt. "I'll never be able to watch another Three Stooges or Laurel and Hardy movie as long as I live."

The front of his shirt was wet with her tears and the streaks of her makeup, but it didn't stop him from holding her tighter and letting her talk. Lord, he empathized with her frustration more than she could possibly know!

"For months she ate her weight in nutritional supplements. Have you ever tried drinking a milk-shake of digestive enzymes and mashed-up vitamins? It's disgusting. It was all so disgusting"— she clenched her fists into the material of his shirt and the skin underneath—"and all so fruit-less."

David bent his head and held it alongside hers, oblivious to the physical if not the emotional pain she was causing him. He held her anyway. He couldn't let go.

"She's been so brave through it all. It's *me* who's falling apart. I don't understand why . . . why?" She pulled back and looked up at him, seeking answers, and was surprised to see that the expression on his face betrayed torment equal to her own. "Why?" she asked him again, the word covering a multitude of questions.

David moved his lips to speak, intending to give

her some of the standard advice learned in his six years of studying psychology. The words stuck in his throat. Think, man! he admonished himself. He had to tell her something, and yet he couldn't bring himself to give her platitudes.

"Dammit!" he muttered. Scott's death had shaken him more than he should have let it, rendering him incapable, for the moment, of being objective enough to help her. "Angel, I don't know why." He wiped a rivulet of makeup and tears from her cheeks, the palm of his hand brushing against her trembling lips as he did so. "I wish I had the answers to give you, but I don't." His fingers stayed where they were, his body responding to the vitally warm life in hers.

She lifted her hands to touch his face, too, her eyes reflecting his own primitive need to embrace life instead of death. Rational thought and cold logic had no foothold in either of their minds just then.

Lowering his head, he ignored the little warning voice in the back of his mind, and brought his mouth down onto hers, licking the moist saltiness of her tears away with his tongue.

Angela responded, directing the passion of her anger into passion of another sort. Their bodies were already touching in sympathy. They moved closer than that now, their motivation changed. The arms that had been cradling her shoulders and back in compassion now enveloped her possessively instead, his hands inflaming rather than soothing.

She clung to him fiercely, seeking to draw his powerful strength into herself. He was a talisman against all the dragon stood for, a living reminder of how things should be. His tall, muscular body felt vibrantly alive. She could feel the strong, steady thump of his heart against her breasts. She could feel the internal heat of him as he exhaled hot, panting breaths of air through his nose, onto her cheeks and lips. And she could feel the virile life force in him as he molded his calves and thighs and hips to hers. Most of all, it wasn't what she *could* feel, but rather what she *couldn't* that drew her to him the most. There was no frailty in him, no need to hold herself back emotionally or physically out of fear of causing him hurt.

After months of holding herself strong and aloof from everyone, it was almost exhilarating to let herself go with someone who gave and took with a fervor equal to her own.

She wasn't the only one feeling intoxicated. David lifted his head from hers for just a second, his expresson bemused, as if just waking up from a dream. Something from the outside world had penetrated his override system and had caught his attention. But what?

His eyes registered recognition then as the knocking on his door was repeated, louder this time. "Just a minute," he called out to the intruder before returning his gaze to the woman in his arms. Disheveled and shaken, her face was tear streaked and her expression was as confused as his own probably was. "It's all right," he whispered. He curled her fingers into one hand and covered them with the other.

All right? Angela asked herself. Whew! She wondered if her face showed the same strange combination of consternation and desire that his did. One moment she had been crying against him;

the next she'd all but been crying *for* him. Face it, she told herself, you've gone off the deep end. . . .

"What is it, Jane?" David thought his voice sounded squeaky, reminding him of the time his father had caught him and a girlfriend on top of his bunkbed. He controlled the urge to laugh hysterically. Angela Newman looked ready to have hysterics for them both.

"I'm sorry to disturb you," Jane called through the closed door, "but there's a Liz Lewis out here to see you. Shall I show her in or ask her to wait?"

"Liz!" Angela made an impulsive move for the door but didn't get far.

"Wait." David held her where she was, in the safety of his arms, reluctant for a number of reasons to let her go. "I don't have time to go into all the details, but Liz has had a difficult few days. You don't want her to see you at less than your best today, okay?" Still holding her hand, he moved to his desk and retrieved some tissues. "Here. Hold still." He wiped her face clean and brushed the hair back from her eyes, noting the puzzlement in her expression. "I'll explain it all to you later." Much later, after he'd come up with an explanation to satisfy himself.

In all the years he'd been studying and practicing psychology, he'd never come close to violating his professional and ethical standards. He exhaled a shaky breath and punched the intercom button on his phone. He'd just come very, very close, if not to violating those ethics, then at least to compromising them. Had he . . . ? Had she . . . ? Had . . . "Jane?" Where the hell *was* Jane? He punched the button several more times before remembering that Jane wasn't at her desk, but rather just outside the door, patiently awaiting his reply. Ye Gods, he was losing all his marbles!

"Jane? Will you please tell Liz Lewis to come in now?"

It took only a few seconds for a fragile-looking little girl with short Shirley Temple curls and enormous green eyes to burst in.

"Aunt Angela!" She catapulted herself across the room and into Angela's arms, and started talking a million miles a minute. "I'm so glad you're here! I just *knew* you'd come if I asked you to. I even told my friend Mildred that you'd come. She has leukemia, too, and we're going to be best friends. I'm sorry if I made you worry by crying on the phone this morning, but I just missed you *so* much and it was a rotten day. I couldn't help it."

Angela exhaled a painful sigh of relief and returned Liz's bear hug with careful enthusiasm. Liz was all right. Whatever David Ortega had done or said, whatever emotional storms Liz had been going through this morning, clearly she wasn't upset now. Except for the dark circles under her eyes and the hollows in her cheeks, she looked and acted like any other nine-year-old. Angela hugged her again for luck. Thank God! They were still holding the dragon at bay.

Liz squirmed free of Angela's embrace and ran over to David, who was seated behind his desk.

"Hello, Liz." He put on his best professional face and tried not to look as though he'd just been run over by a truck. Thankfully he was sitting down. "Don't you think we'd better explain to your aunt about our little talk this morning?"

"Yeah." Her curly head bobbed up and down in sincere apology. "And I promise I will later. But right now I just want to tell you I'm sorry if I got you in trouble. I talked to Sylvia too. . . ." She shrugged guiltily. "I wasn't really mad at you, you know. It wasn't your fault that Scott died or that you told me the truth when I asked"—she shrugged again and studied her feet—"about me. I was just angry at the world. Do you know how that is?"

David rubbed his right leg unconsciously and nodded in understanding. "Don't give it another thought. I know. And I know you didn't mean what you said."

"Oh, but I *did* mean part of it, the *nice* part." Liz turned around to her aunt hopefully. "The part about wanting Aunt Angela to come and stay with me while I'm here at Casa de los Niños." She looked from one adult to the other, innocently unaware of the reason behind their simultaneous gasps. "*You* told me"—Liz looked pointedly at David—"that this was *my* time to have the time of my life, and that you'd do anything in your power to make sure I had fun. And *you* said"—she looked plaintively at Angela—"that *nothing* was impossible and that you'd do *anything* you could to make sure all my wishes came true. Well, all I want is one teensy-weensy favor. I want Aunt Angela to stay, okay?" She shuffled her feet and looked back to David as his telephone rang. "That's probably Sylvia."

"Sylvia?" Both David and Angela echoed the name, Angela with curiosity, and David with dread.

"Weeeellllll . . ." Liz said as David stared at the phone. "I sort of already talked to Sylvia about it, and she said she was going to talk to the director today, and you and Aunt Angela tonight over dinner. She said she was going to call you to discuss the details."

"Wonderful." David clutched the receiver as if it were a snake while Angela gaped at Liz.

Liz smiled in innocent satisfaction. "I'm *so* glad you think so. Really, I wasn't too worried about it. I just knew the two of you couldn't come up with any reasons why you should deny me this one wish."

Two

They both could, and did.

"But princess, I have work to do." Angela went over the arguments she'd used earlier with Liz.

"But you can write your stories and draw the pictures to go with them anywhere," Liz had argued. "You take your notebook and sketch pad everywhere."

"But it's not just the writing," Angela had countered. "You know I have other work to do. The president of a printing and publishing company, even a small one like ours, can't just take two weeks off for a vacation."

"But you're the *president*," Liz had said. "And Mom's got a say in the company too. Who's going to fire you?"

The child had a future as an attorney . . . *if* she had any future at all. In the end Liz had touched Angela's Achilles' heel. "What's more important to you," she had asked, "me or some dumb old job?"

She was going. She was staying.

David took the long way around from his office

to the camp cafeteria where Sylvia and Angela were no doubt already awaiting him. He'd finally and reluctantly agreed to allow Angela to stay for the night. Sylvia wasn't going to convince him to let her stay longer. Hell, Sylvia knew the rules. She'd helped establish the blasted things. It was just that Liz was so persuasive, so ill, even though she wasn't showing it too much yet, and so determined to have only one thing: Angela.

He sympathized. He *empathized*. But it just wasn't possible. Their facilities weren't equipped to handle it; their social programs weren't designed to deal with her; he wasn't able to handle— Well, perhaps that was the crux of it.

He made a quick side trip through the boys' dormitory, ostensibly to see that every child made it out of the cabins and into the cafeteria but actually to give himself time to collect his thoughts before dinner. Sylvia had a nasty habit of analyzing his every word and gesture, and he was pretty sure he didn't want her poking around in his present thoughts. He wasn't sure he wanted to examine them too closely himself. The truth of the matter was that he *was* designed, equipped, and more than *able* to handle Angela Newman. There was nothing wrong with that part of him . . . but the emotional reactions worried him. It had been a long time since he'd responded to a woman the way he had to Angela. The women in his life recently had been—how to put it politely? —temporary in nature. They were professional women, women he'd met at psychology conferences, women who were as much in control of their own emotions as they were their social lives and well-planned careers. He didn't know a one of them who would have allowed herself to throw a tantrum, much less scatter his papers on the floor and then hurl herself into his arms, admitting both weakness and desire. Worse, he didn't know a one of them whom he'd have wanted to behave that way. He was comfortable with the barriers he'd put up, and he didn't like the idea of Angela Newman tearing them down and feeding them to him for breakfast. The solution was simple: she was going, even if it meant he had to call in every favor Sylvia owed him, and put himself in debt to her up to his eyeballs. Besides, the rules were the rules, and they weren't made to be broken. Forcing himself to be comfortable with that rationalization, he strolled into the noisily crowded cafeteria and searched through the long picnic-style tables for a head of windswept hair and a pair of gorgeous green eyes.

Angela sat at a corner table and watched the door, grateful that Liz and her friends were making her own somewhat distracted answers to Sylvia's questions less obvious. She nodded politely and mumbled something vague as Sylvia tried to communicate over the noise and around a sea of bobbing pigtails and scarves. Where was he? There was no logical reason why she should care where he was, but that thought didn't lessen her curiosity a bit. Something had happened between them, something that she might have been able to attribute to her volatile emotional state if not for the strange way she was still feeling at just the thought of seeing him again.

"Oh, this is crazy!" She tore her gaze away from the door and muttered to herself. "You wouldn't be feeling this way if he *had* looked like Sigmund Freud, now would you?"

"Sorry." Sylvia raised her voice to be heard over the din of little-girl voices. "I couldn't hear what you said."

Good thing. Angela moved Liz to a spot on her lap and scooted closer to the psychologist. A roly-poly marshmallow-shaped woman with a benignly cordial expression, Sylvia Krisik gave one the initial impression of being a dark chocolate-brown Mrs. Santa Claus. But there was a shrewd perception behind those friendly brown eyes, and Angela was quite sure she was being carefully scrutinized and weighed accordingly. She didn't want, and couldn't afford, to appear scatterbrained.

"I . . . um . . . said that I was surprised to find this place looking just like a normal, everyday, run-of-the-mill summer camp, very much like the one I went to when I was ten." She looked over to a table of boys across the room. Engaged in a free-for-all food fight, they seemed oblivious, at least for the moment, to their critical illnesses.

"Run-of-the-mill, huh?" Sylvia fingered her double chin thoughtfully and studied the younger woman.

"Well, there *are* differences. . . ." Angela looked at the boys again, several of whom were now sporting globs of mashed potatoes. Two on one side of the table were in wheelchairs, while several more had heads that were as bald as melons. But aside from those physical differences, they were acting like normal boys. "I bet you have panty raids, buckets of water over the door, and frogs in the fruit punch." She tightened her hold on Liz as the little girl giggled. "Any ideas you get at this table, pipsqueak, are to be considered strictly taboo."

Liz stifled bubbles of laughter and her friends hid their faces.

"Don't tell me you've already put frogs in the fruit punch?"

"No," Liz said, but as Sylvia lifted an eyebrow, she hastened to explain, "but they did try an old trick."

Sylvia smiled. "They tried the Ex-Lax in the brownies trick. Fortunately I never eat brownies made by sly little girls." She winked at Angela and sent the culprits into peals of laughter. Chucking one of them under the chin, she shooed them away like a flock of noisy pigeons, and turned her full attention to her guest. "I'm glad to hear you're able to see the positive as well as the negative about these kids and our camp. Many people can't."

"Does that mean you're going to support the idea of my staying for a while?"

"When you get to be my age, you generally learn from experience that it's frustrating, if not pointless, to fight the inevitable." Sylvia cocked her black, curly head toward the door, her eyes full of warmth. "I'm afraid my friend is young enough to be in a permanent state of frustration."

She could have sworn Sylvia hadn't been looking directly at the door, but there he was, Mr. Frustration himself, if his expression was anything to go by. The lips that had so softly caressed hers were drawn into a thin line. The blue eyes that had held so much empathy were unreadable now, and his expression was coldly uncompromising. He held himself stiffly erect, as if control were of the essence. With his long, quick stride, he would have been upon them in seconds if not for the group of food-splattered boys who waylaid him, and the trio of cafeteria workers who followed close behind. It was several minutes before he could extricate himself from their clutches, and when he did so, his "Wanna play doctor" sweatshirt had acquired some new stains.

"Really, David . . ." Sylvia held out a chair for him. "I'll be glad when you finally get that doctorate. Your shirt's disgusting."

A corner of his mouth twitched and he swatted at the muck on his shirt with a napkin. He couldn't carry off the stern act with sweet potatoes and corn sticking to his clothes. "It's not the shirt's fault. I've been slimed."

"The cook wouldn't appreciate your choice of description," Sylvia said teasingly.

"The cook, I'll have you know, dines at Jack-in-the-Box in Ramona." He dipped his napkin into a half-empty glass of water and added a wet spot to the stains.

"Ramona?" Angela spoke to him for the first time since that afternoon, her voice oddly high-pitched. "Isn't that the little town I passed through to get here?"

"One and the same." He lifted his eyes to meet hers, an electric nonverbal communication passing swiftly between them.

"It's a nice little town." Sylvia looked at them both with a clinician's interest. "Now that Angela is going to be staying here for a couple of weeks, maybe you could take her into town and show her the sights."

"There aren't too many sights in Ramona for someone who likes living in L.A.—" He stopped in mid-thought. "Now that Ms. Newman is *what*?"

"Staying," Angela answered firmly, wishing her voice sounded more steady.

David threw a "help me" look in the direction of

Sylvia, who was smiling with all the satisfaction of a cat on a tuna boat. She was going to be no help whatsoever, he thought. "I don't know if staying is such a good idea," David said. "We have rules against relatives staying with their kids. We don't have all that much room to spare, and every mother, father, uncle, or aunt who stays takes a bed away from a potential camper. You wouldn't want to do that."

"Of course not," Angela said. "That's why I plan to go back into town and buy a sleeping bag. I can sleep on the floor in Liz's cabin. I already asked the other girls and they don't mind."

Of course they wouldn't mind, he thought. What was to mind? He wouldn't mind her sleeping in his cabin, either, but there *were* rules. "I suppose you could do that," he conceded. "But we have the insurance to consider. We aren't insured for long-term stays by adults, are we Sylvia?"

"That isn't a problem either," Angela countered. "I can sign a waiver or post a bond, or . . . or . . . whatever. I won't let that be a problem."

"It's already taken care of," Sylvia interjected smoothly. "I spoke to the director this afternoon, and we can take the waiver option."

How helpful, David thought. He was going to get Sylvia for this just as soon as he figured out why she was doing it. "We don't have much in the way of adult entertainment," he warned Angela. "We're set up for kids. You'll be bored to tears within twenty-four hours."

"Mr. Ortega, I don't believe I've ever cried from boredom. If I ever did, I don't anymore. I save my tears for the serious things. I don't enjoy adult games. I'm lousy at them. I much prefer the kind of simple fun there is to be had here. Don't forget, I write children's fantasies for a living, and I like what I do."

"We're not living in a fantasy world, Ms. Newman." He had forgotten Sylvia was even in the room. "We have to deal with reality whether we like it or not. I think you will feel out of place."

"My place is with Liz until she gets better." He wasn't going to intimidate her. She wasn't even sure why he was trying. Could he still be upset about all that paperwork? Or was it just her? Sparks had certainly flown between them right from the first. Yet, she could have sworn they weren't sparks of anger . . . at least not on her side.

"Until Liz gets *better*?" He looked to Sylvia for support. She was eyeing them both with unabashed curiosity, but she didn't look the least interested in helping David. "Ms. Newman, Angela . . ." He cleared his throat. This was the part he hated most, having to convince parents that their children were terminally ill. "I've seen Liz's medical records. That is, I don't think you can hold out much hope for . . ." The stubborn determination on her face didn't crack. "Some things are impossible."

There was that word again. "Not for me," she said simply. "And not for Liz, not as long as I'm here."

She believed it. He could see it. "Some things are impossible," he repeated.

"Not for Liz and me." She wasn't going to believe in the worst. "When I was eighteen, a freak fire in the printing business my family owned killed my parents and Liz's father, and utterly destroyed everything else. Janet, Liz's mother, was several months pregnant. She couldn't work. Her health was precarious. Everyone told me it was an impossible situation." She held her head up high. "I absolutely *hate* that word. I finished high school and worked at two jobs. I started college and worked three jobs. Little by little, after Liz was born, Janet and I started to rebuild the printing business. I finished college. The business grew and expanded. Janet began to write children's stories, as she'd always wanted to. I illustratred them for her and began to write a few of my own. It was easy with Liz around for inspiration. Every time we made up a new bedtime story, we wrote it down. One thing led to another and we started printing them up and distributing them on a limited basis to local stores, and then to bigger stores. Today Janet and I own a business that everyone told us was an impossibility." She leaned her arms on the table and confronted him. "I don't believe anything is impossible anymore. Seeing that you do only makes me all the more determined to stay here with Liz. I don't intend for her to believe in the impossible either."

"Sylvia . . ." He was going to drag his colleague into this. He needed her support. No one advocated telling terminally ill children that they were going to die, but at the same time, you had to be honest with them when they asked questions. "Sylvia, what do you think about all this?" She was thinking something. He could practically see the wheels turning.

"What do I think?" She chuckled and, pushing her ample girth away from the table, got up to leave. "I think I'm surprised that you'd ask what I think since for some reason you have such strong opinions yourself."

"Sylvia," he said in a warning tone.

"Oh, and I think that anybody who's determined enough to promise the director six cases of children's books, free volunteer work for two weeks, and a sizable donation to the program is probably determined enough to accomplish what she wants no matter what anyone else thinks."

Angela hadn't. David looked at a smug Angela. Angela had. She'd bribed the director.

"Besides," Sylvia said, "I think that since Liz is more your patient than mine, that you should give in gracefully, take Angela under your wing, and show her around."

Under his wing? How about over his knee?

"And last but not least, I think the two of you should find some nice, quiet, private place to discuss your . . . ah, differences." She smiled. "Otherwise, some people are going to be asking a lot of questions."

Oh, damn. Sylvia's focus on him and Angela meant he wouldn't be able to open his mouth without having his every word analyzed. "I think it's time for you to say good night, Sylvia."

"Good night, Sylvia!" Her laughter rang out loud and hearty. "And good night, David." She held out her hand to Angela, who took it warmly. "I think this is going to be a *very* interesting two weeks."

David rubbed his temples after he was sure her back was turned, and did his best to ignore the two teenage boys who'd just discovered Angela's presence. Someone up there didn't like him.

"Hiya, doc." A rail-thin boy with short, carrot-red hair wrapped his arm around David's left shoulder. "Whatchadoin'?"

"Going crazy, Eric. And if you don't mind, I'd rather do it in peace."

"You can't do that, Doc." Another boy of about sixteen leaned on David's other shoulder, balancing a pair of crutches against the table. "Docs aren't allowed to go crazy. Besides, you haven't got any cancer, so what do you have to go crazy about?"

David looked up into Angela's amused face. If they couldn't see for themselves, he wasn't about to tell them. "Did it ever occur to you that I might be going crazy because I can't seem to keep my shirt clean in this zoo?" He brushed the cookie crumbs away that Eric was dribbling over his shoulder.

"Naw." Eric plucked at the shirt. "Shirt's got character. I'd even wear it."

"You wouldn't know what to do with it if you had it," his companion mocked. "It's a "Wanna play doctor" shirt. I bet you don't even know what that means."

"Do too."

"Do not."

"I could always take lessons from the doc." Eric leered at Angela. "I bet he gets lots of practice playing doctor, right, Doc?" He leaned forward and batted boyish eyelashes in Angela's direction.

Angela bit her tongue to keep from laughing. Boys. Normal teenage boys with way too many hormones for their own good.

"So who's the honey?" Eric asked David conspiratorially. "One of the new den mommies or your current squee—*EEEK!*"

David loosened his grip on Eric's collar. "Nick?"

He propped the crutches under the boy's arms. "Why don't you take Eric here to the telephone to call his mother? Tell her to buy him some new shirts. This one's so tight it's about to strangle him."

"Right, Doc." Nick grinned and nudged Eric, who had moved just out of arm's reach. "Let's go, bud. The doc obviously has other plans."

The tall Scotch in the privacy of his cabin was looking better and better all the time. He offered Angela an apologetic smile and an olive branch. "I don't suppose you'd be interested in a couple of medium-rare porterhouse steaks away from this madhouse, would you? I can't promise anything too fancy, but I'm sure my fridge could provide something to go with those steaks better than this." He flicked a glob of dry mashed potatoes from his clothes. "Besides that, as Sylvia pointed out, we need to find a quiet place to talk. I think I probably owe you an explanation or two."

Angela hesitated. Why did she have this gut feeling that it would be less dangerous to be on his bad side than on his good side? And why, oh why, couldn't he have looked just a smidgen more like Safe Sigmund?"

"My reputation is greatly exaggerated, I assure you." He flashed her a promising smile. "I haven't played doctor with anyone since the Thompson twins came to camp."

"The Thompson twins?" Visions of double Miss Americas playing doctor with David Ortega between them filled her thoughts and flooded her cheeks with red. Oh, brother, she thought, she was in bad trouble.

"The twins were eight and I was nine, and I bandaged their dolls with half a roll of pilfered tape and a box of surgical pads." His eyes twinkled as he stared at her flushed face. "You must write some fantasies. I wouldn't even try to compete with your imagination."

Did psychologists do anything besides play with people's heads? She glanced at David's all too appealingly masculine body. On the other hand, maybe she'd be safer if he did confine his interest to the above-the-neck portion of her anatomy. "Steaks, huh? Maybe I'll just go find Liz and see if she'd like to join us."

"I think . . ." He reached out to touch her wrist, and felt that same rush of energy he had when he'd first touched her. He let go at once. She wasn't running anywhere. As a matter of fact she seemed to be frozen to her chair. "I think some things are better done without children present," he said softly. "Besides, Liz left for the Fun Center with her friends. If you'd like, we can stop there first on our tour of the camp and you can tell her where you'll be."

She pulled her hand back from his tantalizingly close fingers and nodded. Tell Liz where she was? She was in deep trouble, that's where she was, and she didn't think Liz was going to be able to help her out of it.

"So how big is your camp?" she asked as soon as they were out of the cafeteria.

"Not too big in actual acreage." He took his cue from her, equally grateful that they had something mundane to talk about. "But we try to provide everything the kids might want in the way of traditional camp experiences. We have horses, gentle ones, and riding trails. We have the lake, of course, with boats and fishing and swimming.

We have the Fun Center. I think we'll stop off there first. It has pool tables, video games galore, Ping-Pong, a reading room, several televisions, a computer or two, almost all donated by people who have had kids here at one time or another." He stopped. He was jabbering like a magpie. What the hell was the matter with him?

"You know, I'd planned to donate the books and money even before I found out Liz wanted me to stay." She didn't know why it was so important that he believe her, but it was. "I like to have things my way, and I'm willing to do whatever it takes to make them happen. But I would have gone ahead with the donation even if the director had refused my request."

"I believe you." He did. Anyone with any insight into people could see that she was honorable, and kind, and caring, and sensitive, and beautiful, and desirable, and . . . And if she stayed he was going to be in one helluva tough spot. "I just don't believe you've thought this thing through carefully."

"I don't see how you can say that." She didn't want to argue with him. She wanted to . . . She dismissed the rest of that thought. For now, getting to stay with Liz took priority over everything else. "I know what I'm getting into." But did she where David Ortega was concerned?

"Do you?" He echoed her thoughts. "I wonder."

"Where are we going?" she asked as he veered off the path, taking her in the opposite direction from the sign that pointed to the Fun Center.

"To a place everybody here sees sooner or later." He made his way down a darkened path with ease, as though he knew it well. "I think it's important that you see it sooner rather than later; it may affect your decision to stay or to go."

The hair bristled along her neck, the sound of the dragon's roar almost audible in her ears. "David, I don't think I want to go in there." She pulled back as they approached a group of buildings.

"No one does," he answered grimly. "If you stay, you'll have no choice."

"What is it?" She hesitated at the doorway.

It was a hospital, a minihospital complete with doctors and nurses, shiny state-of-the-art equipment—and the smell she hadn't ever managed to get out of her nostrils in all the months Liz had been with her. The hospital was quiet, still, all white like winter snow.

One of the doctors looked up as they walked in and came over to greet them. " 'Lo, David." He shifted a chart to his left hand and clasped David's shoulder with his right. "Sorry to hear about Scott. I was really pulling for that little guy. I know you were too."

"His parents called you?" David's voice was wooden, as though a machine and not a man was talking.

"No. I called the hospital and talked to the specialist on duty. I confess—" He looked off, apparently finding something of great interest in one far corner that kept him from finishing what he had been about to say. "It's harder with some. So, what brings you here tonight? You're all right, aren't you?"

"Fine." David shook his head emphatically. "I just thought I'd stop by and say hi to some of the kids. I brought a friend." He pushed Angela forward. "Angela." He nodded at the doctor. "Angela, this is Sam, the real doc."

Angela took little steps forward, her legs threatening to turn around of their own volition and leave the dragon's lair. "Pleased to meet you," she said as she shook Sam's hand.

"Nice to meet you too. I'd stay and chat, but I've got a blood workup to check on and some anxious parents to talk to. I'll see you later."

They said their good-byes and David tugged at her hand. "Come on," he said. "There are a couple of kids I need to see."

"Wait a minute." She could feel her heart pounding in her chest, affirming its life force. "Can't it wait until tomorrow? Couldn't you see them then?"

"One of them might not be here tomorrow." His answer was short and choppy. "The other, Benjy, needs to see me tonight." He turned sharply into one room, the lights very dim.

"Hi, there, Benjy." David leaned over the hospital bed and ruffled a small blond head. "How are the headaches?"

"Fine, Doc. They changed medicines again and fixed it." The small boy's voice was high and squeaky. "Do you think they'll let me out to play soccer tomorrow if I tell them it doesn't hurt anymore?"

"I don't know about tomorrow, sport," David answered lightly. "I'm sure you'd do fine, but it looks like rain. In fact, we'll probably have to postpone that game for a few more days."

Angela edged over and closed the curtains tighter so that none of the sunshine-filled day's brilliant sunset could shine through.

"But I'll be able to play when you do, right?" Benjy asked hopefully.

"Yup." David got off the bed. "Even if the coach has to kidnap you and carry you off."

Benjy giggled. "You could get in real trouble for that, coach."

"Yeah." David grinned back. "But I'd be in worse trouble if my star forward couldn't play. So do us both a favor and get better quick, okay?"

"I will, coach." Benjy closed his eyes tight. "I promise."

"Can I do anything for you before I go, Benj?" David whispered.

"Yeah." Benjy cracked one eyelid. "You could turn the lights on *real* bright and break the switch so nobody can turn them off again."

"Break the light?" He frowned. "But Benjy, if I break the light switch you'll have to sleep all night in the light. It's kind of hard to sleep, buddy, with a light glaring in your eyes."

"Not for me," Benjy denied. "I don't like to sleep in the dark, ever. Once I woke up and it was dark and night and I couldn't hear anything, and I thought I'd died and nobody had told me. It was all the way in the morning before somebody came in." He shrugged, his shoulders baby-bird frail. "If it's light I can look around and see whether I'm alive."

Angela shivered uncontrollably as the dragon roared somewhere very close by in her imagination. She stepped forward and wedged herself between David and Benjy's bed. "Hi, Benjy. My name is Angela, and I've come to see you for a very special, special reason."

David looked at her uncertainly. What was she doing?

"I was wondering about you," the little boy conceded. "I haven't seen you before, and you don't look like a doctor or a nurse or nothin'."

"Nope." She swallowed a huge lump in her throat. "I'm not a doctor or a nurse, but, like them, I have come to help you. It's about what you just said was worrying you. I have a solution, one that'll take all your worries away. Do you want to hear it?"

"Sure," Benjy said hesitantly. "As long as it doesn't hurt."

"It doesn't hurt." She sat down on the bed, her mind racing to piece together the fabric of a fantasy. "Did you know that a long time ago everyone had a guardian angel to watch over him, to care for him when he was alone or scared or hurt or in trouble?"

"No." Benjy's eyes filled with wonder. "Honest?"

"Scout's honor. Anyway, there were only a certain number of angels. When more people were born, some had to go without angels. Today, only a very few people are lucky enough to be assigned a real angel."

"Is that why I've never heard of them?"

"That, yes, and because they're invisible. You can only see them when you really need them, or sometimes when you dream."

"I wish I had one," he said wistfully. "I really do need one."

"That's why I'm here." Angela did her best to imitate the voice of a cheerful Disney character. "I'm here to deliver an angel to you."

"You are?" He beamed. "Where is she? Can I see her?"

"If you go to sleep and dream you might see her. But you may not see her at all until you really and truly do need her."

"Like when I die," he said matter-of-factly.

Angela bit her lip. It wasn't *fair!* "I know a way you can see her a long time before then. Would you like me to draw her picture for you?"

Benjy nodded excitedly. "Can you do that?"

"I can if you happen to have any crayons and paper."

He nodded toward a drawer in his bedside table, and David opened it. He took out markers and a notebook.

"Are these okay?" Benjy asked.

"Very good." She proceeded to draw furiously, sending the pens flying across the paper until the drawing was complete. The angel was done in bright golds, reds, and oranges, with a cheery yellow aura and streaks of brilliant sunshine surrounding her wings.

"She's *beautiful*," Benjy whispered reverently. "Does my angel really look like this?"

"I haven't seen her myself because she's just for you, and no one else can see her. But I believe she does look like this, and I'm sure you'll know her when . . . when you see her." Angela bent over and kissed his head. "I gotta go now, friend, because I have other angels to deliver."

She turned and fled the room without waiting for David. Unshed tears made her anguished green eyes very bright. Damn David for bringing her here! Damn the dragon for attacking one so young! Damn it all! She bolted out of the building and broke into a run along the sagebrush- and boulder-lined path.

"Angela!" David's voice called out to her from behind. "Wait!"

Angela felt herself jerked around, but the tears seemed to have misted everything into blurry haziness, and she couldn't see David's face. It didn't matter. As angry as she was with him, she didn't want to see him. He had known how she'd feel seeing that sick little boy. He'd known!

"Don't you say one word!" she screamed at David, who was now holding on to her arms. "Don't you dare tell me those were lies and fantasies and that Benjy has to learn to deal with reality! I don't want to hear it from you! In fact, don't you dare say *anything* to me, David Ortega, or I swear I'll break your face!"

"I wasn't going to say any of those things." He ran soothingly steady hands down the sides of her shaking arms. "I was going to say thank you for making Benjy feel better. If it was a fantasy, I liked it, and it didn't hurt anyone."

"It hurt *me*!" she cried.

"I know." He held her close. "I know, Angela. But don't you understand? You had to see, you had to know that all our kids here at the camp aren't like Eric and Nick, or even Liz, still relatively happy and for the most part not too handicapped by their disease. There are the others, the Benjys . . . the Scotts . . . I'm sorry, but you had to know about them, too, before you could make the decision to go or to stay." He tilted her head up so that their eyes met, the anger draining away from hers to be replaced by that same hungry, desperate need he'd seen there earlier. Sweet merciful heaven, how he wanted her! He needed her, and for probably the same reasons. And for that reason, and others, he couldn't have her.

"Will you come back with me to my cabin"—he loosened his hold on her despite the fact he wanted to give her a bone-crushing bear hug—"just to talk?"

She nodded and let him lead her up to the path and over to his cabin.

As soon as they were inside, he handed her a glass full of pale amber liquid. "Here. Drink some of this."

"I don't drink." She sank down on an old cracked brown leather couch, and pushed the glass away.

"It's not social." He pushed it back. "It's medicinal." He waited until she'd gulped a couple of swallows before leaving her to go to the kitchen.

She watched as he picked up a few items of clothing, probably discarded earlier, and began taking things out of the refrigerator. How could he do that? She looked into the bottom of the glass, noting that she'd consumed almost half of it in two gulps. The potent stuff was even now sending its fiery warmth throughout her body. But her mind was still icy numb, and the thought of eating anything made her ill.

"How long does he have?" she asked in a small voice.

"How do you want your steaks cooked?" David shouted from the kitchen.

Hadn't he heard her? She rose and picked her way past his few austere pieces of furniture on her way to the kitchen. His house was totally unexpected, furnished in what looked to be early garage sale. He had a radio, stereo, and TV, but they were small, old, and looked to be on their last legs, as though he hadn't bothered to maintain them. His kitchen was in the same shape, spare and shabby, but utilitarian.

"I asked you how long Benjy has?"

"I'm going to make a salad. Would you like some beans to go with your steak? I make a great pot of pork and beans."

"David!" She resisted the urge to smash the glass of Scotch on the floor. *"How long does Benjy have to live?"*

He put the knife aside that he'd been using to chop vegetables and pressed his hands to his face for just a second. "Maybe a couple of weeks," he replied softly, so softly she could barely hear him. "His parents will be up to get him on Friday, or earlier if it looks like they'll need to." He picked up the knife again and resumed annihilating the produce.

They were going to have salad puree. Angela drained the glass of Scotch and watched as he put their steaks under the broiler, opened a can of pork and beans, and added spices to the pot. He worked methodically, not speaking to her, not looking at her. If he hadn't stopped to pour the remainder of the bottle of Scotch into her glass, she would have sworn he'd forgotten all about her.

"What?" She raised an eyebrow as he threw the empty bottle in the trash. She was angry and she wanted to lash out at someone. He was handy, and besides, she hadn't forgiven him, wasn't sure she wanted to forgive him for taking her to the camp hospital. "You're not going to join me?"

"No." He put salad on their plates and carried them to the living-room coffee table.

"What kind of a man are you?" She followed him out. "I'm still shaking after two glasses of medicinal booze and you're as cool as a cucumber without any. What's the matter with you? Are you so insensitive that death doesn't bother you, or are you just too tough to admit you need your own remedy?"

He went back for the salt and pepper before he answered, his face hard and masklike. "I've known too many good doctors who started on that sort of medicine and never stopped." He looked at her oddly. There was something hidden in the depths of those cold blue eyes, something he couldn't afford to let out. "And besides, there's not enough Scotch in this entire state to numb some kinds of pain. I've tried it at times like this before and it's like drinking tap water."

She'd gone too far. She knew it in an instant, and she couldn't figure out why she'd set out to hurt him. It wasn't his fault that life had been cruel to Liz and to Benjy. "I'm sorry." Her words were so woefully inadequate.

He set the salt and pepper shakers on the table and went to the couch. "I know why you're angry, and I know what you're going through, which is one of the reasons I think it would be better if you didn't stay," he said before he sat down and motioned to her to join him.

"One of the reasons?" She had a feeling the others didn't involve Benjy or anyone else except her and David.

"One of the reasons. But I think we'll wait to discuss the others until *after* you've gotten something in your stomach. I get the impression that either I've misjudged your body weight drastically, or all that medicinal Scotch was taken on a thoroughly empty stomach." He grinned and indicated with a nod the plates on the table.

Angela took the knife and fork he offered, but made no move to eat a bite of salad.

"Steak will fix you up," he said cheerfully. He rose and went into the kitchen, returning after a few minutes with two plates filled with steak and beans.

"It looks wonderful," Angela said. "But I'm not very hungry. To be honest, I don't even remember when I ate last."

"And I've filled you with liquor." He picked up her knife and fork and cut her meat into bite-sized pieces. "I want you to try some of this, just a few bites. It'll help. You'll see."

Angela was surprised to discover that he was right, and even more surprised when she looked down to find her plate empty. "Why don't you let me help you with the dishes?" She lifted the plates, but stopped when he put a restraining hand on her arm.

"Later maybe." He let her replace the plates, but didn't remove his hand. "Right now I think we need to talk."

"About why you don't want me here." She'd thought all the good food had dulled the effects of the Scotch, but as soon as he touched her she tingled with shivery waves of hot and cold. She felt dizzy and giddy and very much as though she wanted to melt.

"It's not that I don't want you here," he said with conviction. "Far from it. I just don't think it would be a good idea."

"You don't?" Funny, but Liz aside, she was beginning to think it was a marvelous idea. So was taking off his "Wanna play doctor" sweatshirt, and running her fingers through all that thick, gorgeous hair. . . . She blinked several times. Potent Scotch. No wonder she never drank.

David's touch turned into a caress as he made unconscious circling movements on her arm. Lord, her skin was so soft and warm, and the way she was looking at him. . . . He shook himself. *This* wasn't going to help matters any. "Look. About this afternoon . . ." He groped for words. How to explain his instant attraction to her, a feeling so strong that he'd thrown all caution to the winds? "About this afternoon . . ."

"You already said that." She licked her lips and tilted her head back to watch the play of emotions across his face. He was really the most handsome man she'd ever met.

"I did?" He had. He set out to explain again, if not to her, then to himself. "I was at a vulnerable point. A little boy I'd gotten very close to here at camp had just died. When you flew into my office looking so vital and alive, I guess I just reached out to that. I needed you then." He pressed his lips together remembering that first passionate kiss. Then? He needed her now.

Needed? Angela wondered. As in past tense? She parted her lips as his very real and present need transmitted itself to her without words.

"But it's just not done," he murmured. Then he groaned and kissed her upper lip, all the while wondering if kissing only half her mouth constituted a violation of ethics. "You don't get involved with your patients' families," he said against her lips. "And, besides, I can't."

For a man who couldn't, he was doing quite a good job. Angela moaned and pressed her mouth harder against his. Tomorrow she would deal with his reality. For now, she was content to wallow in fantasy with David.

He managed both lips this time. Too late. He *was* involved. There was no couldn't or shouldn't about it. All he could do was resolve not to give in to the feeling . . . much more . . . after tonight. . . .

He exhaled loudly and held her slightly away from him. "Angel, I think maybe I'd better get you to Liz's cabin for the night so you can go to sleep." Alone.

"I can't sleep there," she informed him practically in between a sudden case of hiccups. "I never did get to town to buy that sleeping bag, remember? But that's all right. I can stay here and find someone . . . uh, something to keep me warm." Somewhere out there past the haze of Scotch and kisses reality was lurking, but she just wasn't interested in finding it now. It had been too long since she'd let herself go . . . too long since she'd relaxed. . . . She curled up with her head on his shoulder. "Do you think you could find a place in here for me to sleep?"

A *great* someplace flashed into his mind.

"Like a fold-away cot or an air mattress?"

Those weren't the places. "I'm not going to be able to get rid of you, am I?" He sighed. He wasn't sure he even wanted to any longer.

"Nope," she mumbled.

"You're too idealistic, Angel. I'm afraid if you stay you'll get hurt." He'd given up on moving himself away from her pliant body, but his conscience hadn't gone under yet.

"I don't hurt anywhere." She slid down further onto his chest. Lord, he felt comforting. "But you're too pessimistic," she said softly.

"Maybe." But there were reasons, none of which he cared to explain to an inebriated angel who would be out of his life in a couple of weeks. He sighed as she fluffed his shirt and settled her head on his stomach, her arms wrapped, child-like, around his waist, her legs curled up.

"What am I going to do with you?" he wondered aloud.

"Let me rest here for just a few minutes. I'm *so* very comfortable. I don't want to go yet."

He didn't want her to go either. He ran wistful hands along her shoulders and back, telling himself that it was just to make sure she was warm. He could let her sleep here for a while. He could even close his eyes and indulge in a fantasy that she might do more than sleep. But when the night and its dreams were over, he would have to put some distance between them if she did not. Because as much as he wanted her, he knew that he could never, ever have her.

Three

"Why, Nick, that's beautiful. I mean, that's just *beautifully* ugly." Angela tapped the sixteen-year-old boy's drawing paper on which a ferocious-looking dragon was sketched.

She smiled in satisfaction as she walked around the tables to make a suggestion here and a comment there. There were twenty-seven dragons in all—pinkish-purple ones, awful orange globby ones, tiny insidious ones, and ones that could only have come out of the worst nightmares. There was one for each of the students who'd come to the art class that she'd persuaded Sylvia to let her set up.

"Once you've finished with your dragons, I'd like you to try to draw a knight in shining armor, like the ones in Camelot, someone who's strong and brave and not afraid of dragons."

She waited for the pencils and pens to start scratching paper again before picking up her own sketch pad. Her dragon was there, a replica of the one she'd drawn that first day. But beside it she'd drawn a knight in shining armor. Standing strong and tall, he held a long, wicked-looking sword aloft, its razor-sharp point directed at the dragon's heart. Her knight was muscular and powerful, his physical size and vitality evident even through the silvery chain mail. His plumed visor was open, and all he needed to make him perfect was a face. She experimented with his hair, coloring it a deep, dark brown, longish and wavy, strands of it curling out from his head gear. His eyes were a penetrating, decisive blue, fringed with sweeping lashes. His face was on the narrow side, his jaw square and rock-hard, his mouth an uncompromising line of determination. He looked like the kind of knight women fought for. He looked like—

Good grief! He looked like David Ortega! Since that first night she hadn't been able to get him out of her mind. His kisses thwarted her sleep at night, and played around in the corners of her daydreams, calling to her vivid imagination, daring her to enter fantasy rooms which she'd heretofore avoided. Actually, she remembered very little of that first night, just snatches of things like David covering her with a ratty old quilt that had felt lovingly warm; David cradling her head first on his lap and then on an old blue bathrobe that seemed to be wearing his spicy after-shave. She'd awakened in the morning to the sight of him bending over her on the couch, his eyes fiercely intimate and caring. She'd expected him to take her into his arms until the smell of burning bacon and the sound of Liz's frantic pleas for help in the kitchen pulled him away. But no. She had to have been mistaken about that. Since that morning she hadn't seen one sign that he wanted to hold her. More to the point, she hadn't seen more than a few signs of him. If she was in one place, he was in another, or made a point of going to another. He'd made it obvious that he didn't want to have anything more to do with her.

She stopped and sketched his face a bit differently, adding a little tenderness that had been missing since that first night. She stopped drawing then. Why was she doing this? The man was a casual acquaintance, for goodness' sake, one who had made it perfectly clear he didn't want to pursue any deeper relationship with her, expecially not since she was a relative of one of his patients. So why then couldn't her heart and mind let go of the idea that he was destined to be something more? Why did her body crave just one night with her knight?

Why? Because her knight wasn't really a knight at all, and he wasn't hers no matter what he was, and because she was a stupid, fanciful romantic who hadn't written a decent fairy tale in so long that she was having withdrawal symptoms. She sighed and considered crumpling the knight. It was impossible, even for someone who didn't believe in impossibilities. What kind of lasting relationship could an idealistic, optimistic writer of fairy tales possibly have with a cynical, fatalistic, grumpy shrink who enjoyed rubbing people's faces in life's ugly realities? She was still pondering the question when a multicolored hand tugged at her shoulder.

"What's wrong, Eric?" She refocused her eyes on the teenager. "Are you having troubles with your knight?" Why not? She seemed to be.

"He's not a knight." He corrected her patiently.

"He's a samurai, and he's all done. What do I do with him now?"

Good question. Had she been daydreaming that long? There were other antsy artists in the room too. "That's easy." She raised her voice to get everyone's attention. "And it doesn't involve drawing, so you can stop writing four-letter words on the back of your neighbor's shirt, Nick, and pay attention. Now, I want you all to just close your eyes and concentrate with me." It was an exercise, a fantasy she often shared with Liz, and one she'd wanted to share with these kids since that first night. "I want you to picture your dragon in your mind's eye. Pretend that he's just like the cancer you have. Can you see him?" She paused until a flock of concentrated faces nodded affirmatively. "Good. Now I want you to imagine that the knight you've drawn is going to find that dragon and slay him."

"But I drew my dragon bigger than my knight," piped the voice of one of the youngest children who was quite clearly worried.

"It doesn't matter," she said. "Your knight can find and slay your dragon no matter how small he is. The battle may be long and hard, but he will win because he's stronger than any old dragon. All you have to remember to do is to engage the enemy at every opportunity. No letting your knights rest on the job until the dragons are banished forever. Okay?"

Her eardrums rang with a chorus of okays, followed by a silence of concentration so tangible that she could almost reach out and touch it.

When a large, strong hand reached out and took her by the forearm, for just a moment it was almost as if her own knight had come to life. But only for a moment.

Half dragging her to stand behind him, David clapped his hands loudly and broke the spell she had been weaving. The paper knight slipped from her fingers as the real man after whom he'd been modeled took over.

"I think those dragons are deader'n doornails, gang, so why don't you all put your pictures away? Sylvia's group is supposed to meet at the Fun Center in five minutes for Donkey Kong championship matches. And in case you've all forgotten, everybody who planned to go on the overnight hike with me was supposed to be ready to go by now. So let's move it! Hop to it!"

Angela waited until the last of them had stampeded by before turning on David in annoyance. "You know the hike isn't scheduled to start for another half hour. I wasn't finished with them yet."

"You were finished." His tone was soft but full of warning. "And unless you want your short career as a camp volunteer finished as soon as it's begun, you won't start that again."

"Start what?" What unforgivable thing had she done that he could see from a position that was always on the other side of the camp from where she was?

He stooped to retrieve the knight that had fallen from her fingers. He waved it in front of her face like a red flag. "Having cancer isn't even remotely like a fairy tale, Ms. Newman. These kids don't live in some fantasy world where knights in shining armor can rescue them from their dragons. You don't have the right to build their hopes up for something that can't possibly happen."

There he went again with those impossibles. Ooohhh! She made a grab for her knight before he could get a good look at him. "I don't believe in can'ts and won'ts." The knight deftly evaded her fingers. "And I don't see what just a little hope does to hurt them. Haven't you ever heard of 'Where there's life, there's hope'?"

She circled him as he turned his back on her and shouldered a bright orange backpack. "I repeat—I don't see the harm in hope."

"You don't see because your rose-colored glasses are too thick." He glared down at her, his breathing rapid and irregular. "Don't you realize that it *hurts* when all the hopes and dreams you've come to expect don't come true? Well, let me tell you, it does hurt. I know."

"Excuse me, Mr. Almost Doctor Know-It-All!" She watched as he crumpled the sketch and shoved it in his pants pocket. Now, how was she supposed to get it back from there? "I'm glad to see that all those psychology classes and all those textbooks have given you such a clear insight into how these kids really feel. But, to my way of thinking, until you're a cancer patient yourself, all you've got is sympathy, not empathy. And for your information, since I've spent quite some time with a cancer patient, I think that makes my second-hand opinions every bit as valid as yours. The only thing you've got on me is a license to practice pessimism, and I don't count *that* as an asset!"

David bit his lower lip, whirled, and walked out the door, fully intending to leave her behind. He didn't want to argue with her about it. Winning would give him no satisfaction. "You can think whatever you like, Pollyanna. And you can paint as many dragons and tell as many fairy tales as you want," he said over his shoulder. "Just keep it all in the fiction section, and we'll have no problems with each other." He walked briskly toward a group of waiting children.

"And let the dragon win without a fight?" She ran to keep up with him. "Forget it. And you can also forget about leaving me behind because I'm coming with you."

He stopped at the mouth of the mountain path where the campers were gathering, and spoke to her in a whisper. "Angel, you belong somewhere where you can make all those wonderful fantasies of yours come true, somewhere with paper dragons and make-believe monsters. It isn't your fault, but you aren't strong enough or tough enough to deal with realities like . . ." He groped for an example harsh enough to convince her but tame enough to leave her illusions intact. He'd seen enough dreams destroyed without causing any to break himself. Somebody had to be left to dream. "Like that." He looked toward the children. Loaded down with daypacks, they could have been any other group of hikers had it not been for the support group administering to their last-minute needs.

Angela watched as camp nurses circulated with paper cups full of pills or disposable syringes of medication, rearranged bandages or adjusted artificial limbs for comfort.

"Everybody on this hike could realistically be in the hospital any time in the next few weeks. It isn't an easy hike, even knowing the support people are going to be waiting at the top for us with some of the comforts of home. I'll have kids who are sick, kids who are hurting, kids who are scared. I'll have to deal with it. I've had to tie artificial arms and legs to my belt and carry the owners on my back. And I've cooked many a beakfast to the sound of them upchucking their medicine. It's not pretty, and I don't think you're strong enough to handle it."

Angela suppressed a shiver. "Funny, but I heard the same thing when my parents and brother-in-law died in the fire and I was left to provide for a pregnant, ill sister and later her newborn babies. I must be stronger than I look." And just tons more stubborn. She met his gaze, refusing to back down. "It sounds like you could use someone on this hike just like me. In any case, you're stuck with me. The director approved my request to go on this trip with Liz just this morning." She made straight for a boulder around which the children had piled their packs, and withdrew a pink one decorated with painted teddy bears.

There were times, David told himself, when fair and reasonable had to make way for macho and chauvinistic, no matter what kind of fight he'd have to wage with the director. "You can't come," he snapped at her.

"Watch me." She tossed the bulging teddy bears over her shoulders and cinched them tight.

Watch her? That was the problem. He'd hardly taken his eyes off her every time they were together, and planning his schedule so he wasn't where she was hardly took her off his mind. He'd been looking forward to this hike so he wouldn't *have* to think about her. Maybe then he'd be able to work her out of his system. There was something therapeutic about a long hike, sore muscles, a good sweat, an occupied mind. He could concentrate on nature and the outdoors.

He watched her walk ahead of him up the trail,

her fanny swaying sexily with each step. How good it would be to lay her down somewhere in the middle of all this nature and make love to her until his backside got as sunburned as her half-bared breasts would. He rushed around her to take the lead.

Several hours later, David stood several yards above Angela on a large rock, and waited for her to catch up. The sun beat mercilessly down on them, the temperature well into the nineties. So far she'd unbuttoned one of her blouse buttons for each ten degrees. He wiped the accumulated sweat from his forehead. When they'd started on the valley floor, it had been about seventy. He could hardly wait for them to reach the hundred mark.

His eyes narrowed as she climbed closer, his attention fixed on the teddy bears whose clasped arms formed the cinch strap riding high under her breasts. What would Sylvia say if she knew he was jealous of a couple of painted teddy bears?

"Hey, Angel?" His voice sounded thick and husky. He cleared his throat and tried again. "Angel, do you think you can manage to haul your fanny up here by yourself, or should I radio ahead for a crane?"

"Ha-ha. Very funny," she grumbled as she stumbled over the rough terrain, the sharp rocks and roots digging into her inadequately shod feet while the sage tore at her bare legs. "I'm coming." Why on earth hadn't she worn hiking shoes instead of tennis shoes, she asked herself as she huffed and puffed up the steep incline.

"Can I expect you sometime during this century?" David asked.

She straightened up to reply, lost her footing

and slid sideways back down, losing a good five feet of hard-earned ground. How had he gotten himself and everybody else up there? A hidden trail? That had to be it. Maybe it was this way?

"Angela, don't go that way. Go the other way," David directed.

She ignored him and his dratted voice of experience. If she let him direct her, she'd end up headed back down the mountain, not up where she wanted to go. She chose another direction and ended up surrounded by a giant wall of sage. She picked bits of the clingy plant out of her hair and pulled her gaping blouse together. "Now what?" she muttered angrily to herself.

"If you'd stop talking to yourself and start listening to me, for a change, I'd be able to give you directions."

"I don't *want* your directions," she retorted waspishly.

"How about a hand instead?" He retraced his steps and emerged almost next to her through a hole in the foliage.

"A hand would be nice." She reached out to him over the boulder that separated them. As soon as she got his hand, she was going to employ what little judo she knew to fling him over her shoulder and down the precipice. And then she was going to drop wooden stakes into his thoroughly black heart. And then she was going to feed his nasty, malicious, and disgustingly handsome carcass to the buzzards.

"Give me your hand, and I'll lead you up." He bent toward her.

She lifted her eyes to see his grubby fluorescent orange tennis shoes at her nose level. Oh, the temptation to tie his laces together and watch him fall flat on his smug face.

"Honestly, Angel!" He grabbed her hand and pulled her up the boulder and out of the sage-brush prison, letting her go so fast once she was up there that she nearly fell back over the edge. "For such a light little thing, you have all the grace of a pregnant hippo." He steadied her, but only for a second. Since that first night, he'd made a point of not touching her.

Not that she wanted him to. She shrugged as he let go of her like a hot potato. She didn't want him to touch her any more than he wanted to. Right? *Right*? She prodded her silent little voice of a conscience. Right! On the other hand, there was a lot of middle ground between being inti-mate and being Attila the Hun. She swept past him indignantly and began climbing the moun-tain again.

"Just a minute, Billy Goat Gruff," she said as she grabbed the edge of his camp T-shirt as he tried to pass her again. "Let's discuss this a min-ute." She tried to catch her breath. "I realize that you and I are perfectly healthy specimens of hu-manity, but our charges aren't. We have two good arms and legs to carry us over this junior Mt. Olympus. Some of those kids don't, and you've got them scrambling over rocks the size of Gibraltar. I don't think that's such a good idea."

"I don't hear them complaining," he said.

Maybe they were too terrified to complain. "Of course not. No one likes to disappoint you." In-cluding her, she realized. "But don't you think it would be a good idea to wait to enter them in the Olympics until they're better?"

David picked up a few pebbles and tossed them

out over the cliff's edge. "We've had this conversation before, you know. I've come to the conclusion that we're not going to agree. But for the sake of getting on with the hike, I'll repeat myself. Most of the kids aren't going to recuperate. They're as good now as they're ever going to get. If they don't make the hike today, some of them might not be able to make it next week. I want them to be able to look back on today and say that they made it, and made it, I might add, ahead of you." He started walking again.

She dug a clump of brush out of her socks. "Speaking of me, think what the camp's director is going to say when you are forced to admit that a dozen hikers and one volunteer died of exhaustion along the trail. Think of the lawsuits. Think, please, of my blistered feet." She hobbled along behind him.

"I think you've been living in the L.A. smog so long that it's rotted your mind along with your lung power." He pounded none too gently on the pack on her back. "There. Can you breathe better yet?"

"At least I've forgotten about my feet." She gasped for breath as they walked. "Couldn't you just leave me to die on the trail in peace? Must you beat me to death along the way?"

"You were the one who said you could hack it."

Her and her big mouth. "That's not what I meant, and you know it. I meant— Oooofffff." She groaned and pulled herself over a pile of river rocks that the kids had probably scampered over with ease. This was humiliating. "I can't do this. This is imposs—" She bit her tongue before the forbidden word could slip all the way out. He picked up on it anyway, reading her mind and her expression with aggravating accuracy.

"I thought you said nothing was impossible." He braced his legs against one large boulder and pushed her up the pile of smooth rocks, his hands cupping her bottom through the bright red shorts she wore.

"That was before we set out on this so-called little hike. Little hike, my big toe! This is Mt. Everest. I should have known something was up when you wore pants instead of shorts on a day like this."

"This is Ramona, California. We don't have an Everest here. Where did you learn geography? Black Canyon wouldn't hold a mountain that size, and that's where we are."

"Black like your heart." She tripped over a shrub and landed on her legs. "And my knees tomorrow morning, if I live that long."

"Besides," he continued, picking up the earlier thread of conversation, "you can't judge where we are by what I wear. I never wear shorts."

"I can't see why not." She looked over her shoulder to openly eye his Levi-clad legs. He obviously hadn't fallen onto every rock and thorn bush between here and the camp as she had. "I'm sure you have very nice legs." *Very* nice legs. Try as she would, she couldn't keep her eyes from straying below his belt. Molded to his hips both in front and in back, the frayed and soft material of his pants clung to his thigh muscles, which were damp with sweat and bulging from exertion. And if the slightly worn, slightly more faded bulging outline in the front of his pants was any indication, his legs weren't the only nice things about the lower half of his anatomy.

"Maybe I have knobby knees." Catching his breath at the look of naked hunger in her eyes, he shoved her none too gently onto the next rock. He didn't need this; at least, he didn't want to need this. Did he?

Angela held her breath, excruciatingly aware that he hadn't removed his hands from her bottom and of how that was making her feel. "Do you have knobby knees?"

A part of him wanted to carry on with the sexually exciting game, to invite her to find out, to bring about what both of them wanted. But another part of him cringed at the thought. "Worse than that." He slapped her behind and pushed her farther up the rock just as Liz's sun-flushed face peered down from the boulder above them.

"Come on, Aunt Angela. We're all waiting for you. People are beginning to wonder if you're out of shape."

"Horror of horrors! Out of shape? Me? A fate worse than death!" she responded dramatically. "I'll pick up the pace." She wiped a river of sweat from her brow and redoubled her climbing efforts.

"I am not out of shape," she said, panting as Liz disappeared.

"I'll have you know that any number of people have told me I'm in perfectly fine shape."

"They're lying." David ran the rest of the way up and flopped down onto a rock to wait for her. "You're out of shape, out of breath, out of sorts, and almost out of time. We're due at the mountain camp in an hour. And if we don't make it there on time, they will get worried and send a rescue team down for us."

"Wonderful." She hauled herself over the final

hurdle and lay there on her stomach, her muscles too sore to move no matter what he threatened.

"Here. Drink some of this." He handed her a half frozen carton of fruit juice from his pack. "Slowly, please. You've made a big enough mess of my life without throwing up on my stuff as well."

"If your life's a mess, don't blame me." She slurped the juice thirstily, a scowl competing with the trail dirt for dominance of her face. "You've only known me a few days, and most of that time you've been avoiding me like the plague." Had she just admitted that she'd been keeping track?

"It hasn't helped much," he complained. "I've been confronted hourly with the results of your Tinker Bell presence. You've got half the kids in camp believing that all they need to get better is a little pixie dust." And she had him almost believing that fantasies could come true.

"Yes, well, we've already discussed how much you dislike my outlook on life." She smashed the empty juice container against the rock, taking her physical and mental frustrations out on stone and plastic. "In fact, come to think of it, from the sparks that fly every time we're together, I get the distinct impression that you don't like anything about me." She stuck her face close to his and glared at him.

"Not true, Pollyanna." He aggressively invaded her personal space, pulling her up so that they were kneeling chest to chest. "As usual you have the facts backward. The sparks don't fly because I like so little about you. They fly because I like— and that's putting it mildly—so much about you!" He was breathing heavily into her face, so intent upon setting her straight that he wasn't even aware of what he'd admitted.

"Even my pregnant-hippo waddle?" Her ego was still smarting from that.

He lowered his gaze to her white blouse. The sweat-dampened fabric clung to the swell of her breasts. His hands ached to do the same. "Especially your out of shape but oh so shapely shape." His muscles and willpower seemed to sag at once. He lifted his arms slowly and brought her close.

Muscle fatigue. That's why she felt like she was frozen to the spot. That had to be why she was in the arms of the very man she'd contemplated throwing off a cliff just minutes ago.

He stroked the back of her head with trembling fingers. He had to hold her for a few moments. If he didn't hold her, he was going to go stark raving mad. No, madder, crazier. The thought of holding her like this had been driving him crackers for days. He couldn't, shouldn't, mustn't. And yet here she was in his embrace. He ran his hands down the graceful curve of her neck, extending his reach to her back, stroking the aching muscles there until he heard her moan in pleasure. He buried somewhere deep inside him the reasons why he shouldn't touch her and proceeded to do what his body demanded. She was even better than the fantasies he'd created about her.

She was all fire and warmth, from the ends of her hair that glinted golden in the sun, to her satiny skin, flushed and hot from the heat of the day and from her response to him. Unable to stop himself, he chased a trickle of sweat down the side of her neck to the valley of her breasts, and caught it with his tongue before it disappeared into the lace of her bra. He felt her shiver of awareness and desire, and kissed away the goosebumps that followed. Stilling her trembling with his own shaking hands, he eased them both down onto the rock until they were half reclining, and hidden from above by the pungent brush. He should have known that this was inevitable. He'd seen too much death to pretend that her life and vitality held no appeal for him. It wasn't fair to her. She was too vulnerable now. But oh, Lord, so was he. He needed her. Could she be right? In her own way, could she really slay dragons and summon angels and fulfill fantasies?

Angela closed her eyes and let the sensations take over, no longer trying to fight or deny them. He was better than any fantasy she'd ever created, sketched, or written about. A dark knight, with moods and depths to his personality that she couldn't begin to understand yet, he in no way resembled the Prince Charming or any of the other men she'd once envisioned herself with. He was different. And it was obvious to her that this was one time when the reality was far and away better than the fantasy. The feelings she'd experienced when they'd first met came back even more intensely. She felt her knees melt out from under her as she gently slid to the rock, his strong arms under her, supporting her and molding themselves to her as if that's where they belonged. The moments passed in sweet oblivion as he brought his lips into intimate contact with hers, their mouths telling the truths that their vocal cords could not.

He freed his hands from her back several seconds later and held them from the temptation of her body. It was something of a shock to realize that they were both still fully dressed. Except for the telltale ache in his groin, he felt as intimate with her as if they'd just made love.

Angela's eyes widened into pools of emerald desire as the same thought occurred to her. She couldn't even try to look away from him in an attempt to hide her thoughts, the mental pictures she'd created as obvious as the graffiti on the rocks they sat on.

Just a few moments more, David promised himself, setting a time limit to the indulgence. He brushed the fine tendrils of curly damp hair off her forehead and licked her salty tasting skin with his tongue. The murmur of desire that escaped her throat spurred him on, stopping the clock. He moved his mouth around to tease her temples first, and then her eyelids, and then her mouth again, making love to it more gently this time. Leaving her lips, he kissed just the tip of her nose once, twice, and then three times for luck before he remembered that he didn't believe in luck anymore. How had she managed to do that? And, where had she been a year ago?

She reached up to thread her fingers through his thick, dark hair. Suddenly it no longer mattered where she'd been a year ago. She was here now, her body soft and pliant and seemingly built to his specifications.

They didn't speak, their bodies too busy exploring forbidden territory, land that had, up until now, been off limits. Those limits grew hazy as the small spark of need they'd allowed to run free grew and expanded to engulf them both. With bodies pressed together in silent celebration, neither one of them heard Liz's exasperated voice calling down to them until she'd called them three times.

"Aunt Angela? David? What *are* you doing down there?"

David caught at Angela's hand just as she was about to run her fingers down from his backside to his thighs and lower. His fingers were still entwined with hers, but his hand held her away from him, the mood broken.

"Ummm, Liz," she called, having trouble with coherent speech. "David was just helping me find the trail."

And helping himself to another helping of disappointment. He carefully extricated himself from her and held himself stiffly away, a shiver of cold running the length of his spine despite the warmth. "Tell the others we'll be right there."

"David, what's the matter?" She looked for the man she'd glimpsed under the armor, but she couldn't find him. This knight was in full battle dress.

"They're going to call out the rescue team, that's what's the matter."

"Yeah," Liz's voice added as a postscript. "Any time now."

Angela sent a baleful glance up through the hedge. She was going to wring that child's neck, niece or not.

He cursed himself for getting them both into something that was going to be sticky to get out of. "For a few minutes, Angela, I conveniently forgot that while you may be Pollyanna, Mary Poppins, and Tinker Bell all rolled into one, I don't believe in miracles, I can't fly, and I stopped being Peter Pan over a year ago."

"I don't understand." Those three words were fast becoming an unwanted personal motto. She didn't understand about Liz or dragons in general or white knights who could change color in an instant to black.

He looked at her hungrily for another long moment before beating his desires back into submission. He could never live up to her fairy-tale expectations of him, and he would be a fool to think she might live up to his. And he wasn't a fool. Not anymore. He didn't dream unrealistic dreams . . . often. "Not even you can sew *my* shadow back on, Tinker Bell, and it's pointless to try."

Angela's expression became grim. Pointless sounded a lot like impossible. Somewhere under all that dark, cynical reasoning, under the layers of Sigmund Freud and logic she had caught a glimpse of a white knight just like the one she'd drawn to banish the dragons. Finding him again wasn't pointless. Finding him was fast becoming an obsession.

Laughing to herself in renewed confidence, she tossed a handful of imaginary pixie dust at his back and followed him up the hill.

Four

"Pixie dust, smixie dust!" Angela grumbled wearily and wiped at her filthy forehead with an equally grubby bandanna. The thick layer of dust covering her entire body had nothing to do with the magic she'd hoped to work on that slavedriver of a white knight. On the contrary. He'd come charging up just as she reached the rest of the group, and before she could do so much as wave a magic wand over his head, had put her to work like a common serf gathering rocks for a fire ring and wood for the fire. She hadn't seen him since.

What kind of a rotten knight would do a thing like that? She dampened one corner of her shirt in water from her canteen and used it to wipe some of the grime from her face. It left muddy circles under her eyes that made her resemble a raccoon. So what was she going to do next? She sank down onto the pile of rocks she'd lugged from what felt like a hundred miles away to think. What she needed was a fairy godmother with the power of levitation. What she really needed was a backhoe and dump truck. What she needed was a psychiatrist to check into her sanity for volunteering for this abuse.

Poof! That *would* have had to have been her third wish. She jumped up in annoyance as her third wish plunked a straw hat down onto her head, and proceeded to delve into the inner workings of her mind.

"Are you crazy or just suicidal?" David bellowed unprofessionally. "I realize that you don't acknowledge the real world, and I know you aren't big on seeing things as they are, but even *you* can't ignore sun stroke."

The hat was several sizes too large, smelled like decaying fish, and looked like he'd used it to store bait. In an explosion of temper, she snatched it off and threw it down on top of the rocks at her feet.

"That was my best fishing hat," he exclaimed.

His best! "You need a new hat. Badly."

He bent to pick up the hat, folding it back into its comfortable, familiar shape before turning his speculative gaze on her. He tried and failed to keep the amusement from his face.

"So do you, Cinderella. You need a whole new wardrobe." Two intriguing circles of dust decorated her chest where her breasts had brushed against the dirty rocks more than the rest of her had. And patches of sweat made interesting shapes under her arms and at her groin, a sensual inkblot test that he'd love to consider in further detail if only things were different. But they weren't, and they wouldn't be, and that was that. He frowned at the opportunity that could never be realized. Even under a coating of topsoil she was easily the most desirable Tinker Bell he'd ever met.

Angela picked up on the frown, if not the reason behind it. "That's not *my* fault." She plucked the dirty clothes away from her sticky body, unaware that he was wishing he could do likewise. "You're the one who put me on the work detail at hard labor."

He looked down at the fruits of her labor, seeing what she'd done for the first time. "Shades of the sorcerer's apprentice." He bent to pick up six or seven of the bigger rocks. "Angel, I wanted enough rocks to make a fire ring, not enough to pave a two-lane highway between here and the valley camp. All we're going to cook is a few hot dogs on sticks and maybe warm some pork and beans." He nodded to the stack of wood she was standing next to. "And we don't need enough fuel to cook Paul Bunyon's ox Babe. Grab some of those big roots and some smaller stuff for kindling. That should hold us until we can send someone back here with a logging permit to get the rest."

"Very funny." She harumphed along behind him, her irritation diminishing with each of his poorly disguised chuckles. Black knights never allowed themselves the joy of humor, did they? David was finding her zealousness almost hysterically funny. Maybe some of that pixie dust had reached him after all.

The camp, when they reached it, was entirely set up with tents, portable bathrooms, and showers. The only things missing were the fire rings and the children.

"Where are the little bundles of energy?" she questioned. "Jogging around the block?"

"Gone swimming with the rest of the volunteers." He stopped next to a big oak tree that had two tents, side by side, under its massive limbs. One of them bore the Casa de los Niños logo. The other looked suspiciously like the one she'd purchased in Ramona earlier. "Leaving me to put up tents."

Angela looked from one tent to the other, noting that there wasn't more than six inches separating them. The man was as convoluted as one of his abnormal-psychology books. On-off. Hot-cold. His feelings for her seemed to change with each breath. One minute he was holding her and the next holding out on her. One moment wanting her, and the next orbiting like some frozen and distant planet, never warm, never touching, but always there. A knight, yes, but one who was white on one side and black on the other. And the hard part was that she never knew which one she was confronting, or why he should be that way. He was a lot more complicated than a fairy-tale hero.

It was unsettling. Heroes, in her books, were all white knights, strong and chivalrous, courtly and gentle. She'd tended toward the predictable and safe variety when choosing the real men in her life too. She liked always knowing where she stood. She liked always being in control. Up until now she had never wanted anything more. Up until now. But her fantasy heroes had never made her skin feel like it was on fire or her blood boil with desire like David did. They had never made her lose control in anger or in passion. No man, real or imagined, had ever done that, except David.

She blinked and shook herself free of the insights she didn't want to see, only to find herself staring right into the eyes of the man who'd brought them all about.

"Whew!" He whistled long and low and raised suggestive eyebrows. "I'd love to have a front-row seat to your imagination. Where do you go when you space out like that? What are you thinking of when I see you looking at me that way?"

She stifled the impulse to tell him. What was the use of trying to convince this real flesh-and-blood hero that it was all right to fantasize a little, when the pragmatic, down-to-earth side of him didn't want to hear it? "I was just wondering what else you'd come up with while you were rummaging around in my things."

"This." He grinned wickedly and held up the scraps of a bikini. "And I had permission to rummage by proxy. Liz said you had nothing to hide." He looked from the suit to her and back again, an impish gleam in his eyes. "I hope she's right for your sake because nothing is exactly what this suit is capable of hiding."

Angela groaned and tried to remember if she had packed an extra T-shirt in her pack to act as a cover-up. The bikini *was* far more revealing than her usual suit, left back in L.A. But it was the best Ramona had to offer, the folks in Ramona being avid sun worshippers. And it had seemed all right when she'd bought it, but now . . . "I probably won't wear the suit today anyway."

He rubbed the bikini fabric between his fingers, wishing he had the willpower to stop their game. He didn't. The bikini, and the thought of seeing her in it, had used up his small supply of willpower. "I think that's a fantabulous idea." He'd had to invent a word to convey how good an idea he thought it was. The usual descriptives didn't cut it. "But I think the camp board of directors might frown on you skinny-dipping in front of the children. Of course if you'd care to wait until dark, I'd be happy to supervise your midnight swim and make sure you didn't get eaten by the fish." He could indulge in this game, he told himself. She wasn't going to take him up on it. He could tell by the beet-red color on her face.

"David Ortega, stop it before I belt you with something heavy!"

He winked at her. "Actually, I came to find you earlier because I was hoping you'd like to go in swimming with Liz." He paused for a fraction of a second. "I won't be going in the water and I'd like to have an adult go in, one on one, with her until we see how she does."

"Sure." She took the bikini from him and slipped into her tent. "Just give me a minute to change."

"I'll tell her you said yes," David said. He sauntered away from the tent where she was undressing before his feet decided to do a number of their own. "Just follow the trail down to the water," he called out to her. "You can't miss us."

He was right about that not missing them part. She couldn't have missed him, her eyes drawn irresistibly to him from the moment she entered the small pond. For one thing, while everyone else was up to their necks in pond water, he was alone, in all his half-naked glory, at the water's edge. Still wearing his denims and the ever present tennies, he had removed his shirt altogether.

She sucked in an appreciative breath as she ogled him from afar. His shoulders were broader than she'd first guessed, his chest wider and cov-

ered with a mat of dark, sensuously curling hair.
How would it feel to run her fingers through it, to
bury her face in the warm, damp muskiness of
his chest, and to breathe in the scent of him?
How would it feel to be boiled alive in the pond
water that felt like it was already steaming because of her thoughts?

Not good. Time for a cold shower. Time to put
her mind on the real reason she'd come to Camp
de los Niños. Liz. She swam with quick strokes
over to the laughing group of girls of which Liz
was a part, and for the next hour did her best to
concentrate on them instead of David.

She'd never realized how easy it was to do two
things at once before. Tossing schools of giggling
little girls high into the air and down into the
water, she still managed to watch David as he
organized a swimming contest. As involved and
as excited as an Olympic coach, he advised on
strategy, tucked bandages in swim caps, and held
on to a myriad of scarves, hairpieces, and artificial hardware as their owners swam from the dock
to a raft in the middle of the pond. She threw
rings out for the girls to bring back and watched
as David leaned out over the dock's edge to clasp
winners and losers alike to his chest. The water
from their bodies drenched him to the waist. And
the sun caught and glistened off the droplets,
dressing his naked chest in light. The sight of his
body and the sound of his laughter filled her with
a poignant longing like nothing she'd ever known,
making her wish he'd clasp *her* to his naked chest
and . . .

". . . teach her the Dance of the Sugarplum
Fairies."

Angela coughed and sputtered as Liz and her

following of splashing water babies dog-paddled over.

"Remember how last summer you taught me to do the Dance of the Sugarplum Fairies in the pool at home?" Liz tugged at her bathing-suit bottom in an effort to gain her full attention.

Angela pulled the bottom back up and the high-riding top down. "I think so, princess, but it wasn't really a dance. It was more of a water ballet, but simple." She tore her eyes away from David and focused them on her niece. "It wasn't anything special."

"It *was* special," Liz contradicted. "And I want you to teach it to my friend . . . *all* my friends."

Angela hesitated, thinking of all the dramatic twists and bends. Maybe her bikini hadn't shrunk while she was in the water, but it felt like it had. "I don't know about that."

"Oh, *please,* Aunt Angela! It would be so much fun," Liz wheedled.

It was such a small request. "Okay. Just a few moves."

The water polo game and David's coaching went kaput then. Within just a few minutes he didn't even have to pretend to keep an eye on the opposing teams. Everyone ten and under was far too busy making fun of the girls' water ballet. Everyone older than ten was . . . Everyone, young and old alike, was going back to camp, David said firmly to himself. It was time for them to rest before dinner, or to wash up before dinner, to make dinner, something.

Once sure that he was the only admiring male on shore, he allowed himself the luxury of watching her unobserved. In a society where being tanned was synonymous with beauty, she stood apart. Dwelling in her castles in the air must not have exposed her to much sun. She hadn't managed to acquire the bronze look. Her skin was a pale, creamy peach that looked as soft as rose petals. The sun had tinted her shoulders and nose a lighter version of red than her suit, had no doubt brought out a few more freckles, and the pond water had plastered her hair to her head. And yet, she still looked like one of the ethereal characters in her own books. He watched with longing as she moved gracefully through the water with her following of preadolescent water nymphs. She extended one long, slim leg here, and the other there, pointing her toes and her fingers in time to a music all her own, shifting and moving in fluid harmony. Her arms told another story, alternately reaching out as if for the stars and then coming back as though to enfold her in a lover's embrace.

Just watching made him want to join her in the dance and spin them both away to the beat of another rhythm.

Angela straightened her bikini top as the dance ended, allowing herself to come back to earth. That *had* been fun. "All right, chickens." She smiled and patted several of the tired heads. "Everyone out of the water."

"Aren't you coming too?" Liz yawned widely, and wiped water from her face.

"In a bit," she promised and lay back in the water to float. "I need to recuperate. You sugarplum fairies gave me a workout."

Actually the reverse was true. Getting into a fantasy had always rejuvenated her. Perhaps that's why she wrote them all down. It gave her a sense of security to know that she could always escape to a place where no one could follow, where no one could touch her—

"David Ortega, you miserable wretch!!" Angela sputtered to her feet in frozen rage, knowing even before she opened her eyes that one person *had* touched her . . . with the rest of the ice from his cooler. "How *could* you do that? That's cold!" She glowered at him with chattering teeth.

"It was easy." He lifted the ice chest high again. "Wanna see me do it a second time?"

"You do and you'll eat your ice chest," she warned.

"Sorry." Actually he wasn't sorry at all. "But I had to get your attention somehow. You didn't answer when I called you."

"You dumped ice water over my head just to get my attention?" She let him haul her out of the water, but reluctantly.

"You have to admit it worked. But that's not why I did it. I wasn't thinking of getting your attention so much as getting your reaction." He held her just far enough away from him so that he could see her cold-stiffened nipples, clearly visible through the thin bathing-suit fabric. He groaned and covered his face in mock shame. "I spent the afternoon watching Nick and Eric ogle the girls. What can I say?"

Angela tried and couldn't quite manage to look mortally offended. "You could say you're sorry like you mean it."

"I couldn't do that," he admitted huskily. "I've been watching you watching me since you stepped into the water some three hours and twenty-seven minutes ago." He double-checked a Rolex at his wrist. "It's a real tribute to my professional objectivity that I didn't send everyone back to camp three hours and twenty-six minutes ago."

Angela tugged at the tiny triangles of red bikini that were all of a sudden too small to accommodate her heavy breasts and taut nipples. "Everyone's back in camp?" When had he done that?

"You mean you didn't notice?" Of course he knew she hadn't.

She'd been too busy watching him and thinking how good it would feel to be held in his arms. He took her there gently, making her wonder if he really *could* read her mind as easily as he seemed to be able to.

Tilting her head back in an almost audible request, she waited for the wished-for kiss. When it came, it was everything she'd yearned for and then some. It left no doubt that this was a real, live flesh-and-blood man. Even her imagination wasn't that vivid.

His lips moved over hers possessively, demandingly, giving and taking with the same hungry need that controlled her. Their mouths opened to each other at the same time, their tongues seeking and finding, their movements unrehearsed but synchronized, as if they both had the same need. Angela could feel tingles of electricity wherever he touched. And he could feel a fire in his blood as she moved with and against him, an aching in his loins that wouldn't be assuaged by either his logic or her fantasy.

"Dear God, I need you!" Never taking his hands from her body or decreasing their pressure, he moved them from her buttocks up to her hips and waist, along her ribs to her breasts and shoulders until finally he reached and cupped her face.

She could feel the passion of his breath on her

skin, could sense the intensity of the emotions behind the passion. There was a great deal more to this man than met the eye. More than she was sure he wanted her to know. And yet the intimacy she'd already shared with him demanded nothing less than a full sharing of everything.

"What *is* it?" She looked up into eyes dark with misgivings and doubt, pressing on only when she saw the barest flicker of hope. "Tell me."

The silence lengthened between them as he struggled with his own private battle. The quiet allowed other, heretofore ignored sounds, to intrude.

His eyes flickered to another spot on the beach farther down.

Her ears caught pieces of a conversation, an argument in progress.

He sighed and caressed her cheeks for a moment, his decision still not made. It would have to be postponed. "It looks like duty calls," he explained softly. "I think Nick's giving Sylvia a hard time and I think I know what it's all about."

Angela was not feeling philanthropic. Desire for him still clouded her judgment, dulling her usual goodwill. "Can't you just this one time stop being so damn professional? Can't you let Sylvia handle it, whatever it is?"

"Not this time." His eyes narrowed as Nick's young voice added its shrill whine to Sylvia's fast-losing-patience tones. "This is out of Sylvia's league."

But not his. "Can I help?" she asked, figuring that if she couldn't beat 'em, she'd join 'em. She fell in beside David as he hurried toward the combatants.

"It's out of your league, too," he said, shaking his head.

"But not out of yours?"

"There's a silver lining to every dark cloud," he answered her enigmatically. "Nick's problem is, fortunately or not, right up my alley." He quickened his stride to reach them.

"Giving the lady a hard time, Nick?" He maneuvered himself between the boy and Sylvia, motioned Angela to stay behind him, and faced the angry teenager.

This was no class clown, no jovial teen who teased everyone unmercifully and threw mashed potatoes at the cafeteria walls in good-natured fun. The young man was clearly enraged and didn't care who knew it.

"I can't give the ladies anything anymore, and I think it's crummy of you to joke about it!" He flung himself down onto the soft ground and lowered his head to his hands. "Everyone's been making cracks about me," he cried in impotent fury. "Some big swimming star I am—can't even swim across a therapy pool without two guys to keep me from drowning, let alone a pond." He lifted bright eyes to David's face, rubbing the traitorous tears away roughly. "I *hate* them. I hate this stupid camp, and I hate everyone here. I want to go home and I want to go now."

"Why?" David knelt beside him. "So you can give your parents and brothers and sisters a hard time? So you can try to make your teachers and friends all miserable and guilty for being healthy when poor little you has cancer?"

Angela gasped in instant outrage. The white knight had obviously retreated somewhere else.

Nick was hurting, and all David could do was rub salt in the open wounds?

"*You* don't understand!" Nick ground the accusation out. "*You* don't have cancer. I do. And not just any cancer. Oh, no. I have to have bone cancer. I could live with leukemia, but not this . . . and not *these*!" He threw his crutches across the beach and into the pond, and pulled his pants up to reveal legs that stopped just below the knees. He pounded on the metal and plastic and fiberglass legs. "I'm a freak! I'm a—"

"You're alive!" David shook him figuratively and literally to his senses. "And if you weren't such a coward, you'd appreciate that fact. There are whole cabins of kids here who'd trade places with poor you in a minute. They'd give up both legs, both arms, and practically anything else just to *sit* in the water, and you're bitching because you don't think you're going to be able to win any more competitions! If you had half their gumption, you wouldn't be crying to run home. You'd be out there trying to swim!"

"You don't have any right to talk to me that way!" Nick wailed.

"If I don't," David roared right back at him, "then nobody else has either. Everyone else is too busy feeling sorry for you to give you the kick in the pants you need!"

Nick's lower lip quivered and Angela started forward, every maternal instinct Angela possessed incited to protection. "This has gone far enough," she muttered to Sylvia.

"You don't understand," Sylvia said, her expression revealing deep admiration.

"I can't hobble around on dry land and be

happy." Nick pleaded with David for understanding. "I *have* to swim."

"Then do it," David ordered.

"I *can't* with these hunks of garbage on." He pounded the artificial legs again as if in breaking them he could release his own trapped limbs which felt as though they were still there, which they weren't.

"Take them off." David's voice rumbled with confidence, as if he had the power to heal. "You don't need your prosthesis for swimming; only for walking. You *can* swim again, Nick, but only if you're willing to try."

"Right," the boy snapped back sarcastically. "And as soon as I hit the water, I'm going to sink like a stone."

"You won't once you learn a few basic movements, practice and rebuild your muscles."

"And how am I supposed to do that?" He glowered, still not wanting to hear anything less than a perfect solution. "If every time I get in the water everybody looks and laughs at the legless freak?"

"Everyone here has something someone else could laugh at. That's no excuse."

"You don't," Nick pointed out. "Sylvia doesn't. *She* doesn't." He nodded to Angela. "You guys see kids like me all the time. You're used to it. *She* isn't. And if you think I'm going to take my clothes off in front of *her* and crawl like a tadpole into the pond, you're nuts."

"I'll leave." Angela started to go.

"No." Sylvia stopped her. "I think you're supposed to stay."

"I'm nuts then, buddy." David's attention was still directed to Nick. He bent down and unstrapped the prosthesis. "Because you're going into that water and you're going to swim if I have to tie you to my back and swim you across the pond myself."

"No, David." Angela broke away from Sylvia. "Don't do this to him."

"I have to." David unstrapped the other leg strap. "For him, and for me."

"I don't want her to see me." Nick refused to look at Angela, ashamed of his body.

Angela whirled around only to have David turn her back around.

"You're not alone, buddy. But she's going to see both of us. No one can hide from reality forever. C'mon."

"Yeah," Nick said spitefully. "If I looked like you, I'd let her see me too. But I don't. *I don't have any legs!*"

"You're not likely to be chosen Hunk of the Month this year," David agreed. "But you've got legs; parts you were born with, and parts you've acquired. But they're all yours. And you've got guts. And I've got your word that you'll try to swim. So let's get this show on the road."

"I didn't say I would," Nick said as David carried him to the water's edge. "I said I would *if* I looked like you."

David set the boy down and looked over to Angela, his expression so vulnerable and intense that it made the hair stand up on her neck. David sat down next to Nick and pulled off one orange tennis shoe. Lifting his right pant leg up, he took a folded piece of paper from his sock and smoothed it open, staring at it a moment before setting it aside.

Angela picked it up as it floated on the breeze. It was her white knight in shining armor, the one with David's face sketched inside the visor. She looked at David, sudden realization dawning in her mind. Dear Lord!

"I'm afraid you *do* look very much like me, Nick." Standing on one foot, David removed his right tennis shoe and let it fall, along with its artificial foot, to the ground. "I'm afraid we're both knights in tarnished armor." He half smiled at an astonished, open-mouthed Nick. "Well, come on. Strip down to your skivvies and let's get in the water. *I* haven't done any swimming myself in the past year, and I'm going to need all the help your arms and legs can give me or we're both going to drown."

Angela sat down on the grass next to a silent, smiling Sylvia and watched as David swam across the pond with a possible future swimming star clinging to his broad shoulders.

Five

Sylvia drew her away to let the two swim alone. "Sometimes you must let them fight their own battles before you step in to help them."

Angela started back up the trail with her, looking back every few seconds to assure herself that David and Nick were both still afloat. "Tell me . . . tell me about . . . ye gods, where do I begin?" She paused and looked out over the pond again, wanting to know so many things that the words crowded her mind for space on her tongue.

"About David and his missing piece of leg, and why he didn't tell you himself before now, and why only a few people at camp know, and how and why it's colored his attitudes about everything else, and why it's made him such an exceptional counselor for our kids?" Sylvia looked askance at her companion. "Tell you about all that when you're not paying the least bit of attention to me?"

Angela tore her gaze away from the pond and focused on the path ahead. The magnitude of the information she sought wasn't lost on her, and yet she *had* to know. And Sylvia knew she did. In addition to being an optimist, Angela was also acutely intuitive, and not at all shy about digging for the facts to support her insights. "Sylvia, it's important. I'm not asking out of idle curiosity."

"Never thought you were." Sylvia's reputation for keen perception was a well-deserved one. "But you see, I have a problem with discussing my friend David. What I know ranges from doctor/client confidences to secrets between friends to camp gossip to mere speculation. Some of it would be unethical to share with you. Mostly I think that if I told you then you'd lose the opportunity of finding out for yourself. And David would not only lose his trust in one friend but he'd lose the opportunity to learn that there are other women in the world he can trust. Do you see?"

"I see that I'd probably get more answers talking to myself," she grumbled in frustration.

"That might not be a bad idea either." Sylvia raised a pudgy hand in salute and headed for the smell of cooking food. "I can tell you that David has good reason to be cautious in his dealings with women. If he ever trusts you enough to let you inside, you'd better be sure beforehand that you can deal with what you find. I wouldn't want to see him hurt again."

Angela refused to be politely dismissed. Sylvia wasn't going to get away *that* easily. "Just a minute, Sylvia." She followed her back to camp and helped dish up hot dogs, beans, and fruit salad for the children, talking as she worked. "Don't let my occupation and outlook on life mislead you. I've seen reality. I've dealt with it intimately. Do you really think I could run a publishing company like mine and be blind to what's going on out there in the real world? No!" She plopped a spoon of pork and beans onto another waiting plate, sending sauce flying everywhere in her frustration. "Sorry," she told the primary wearer of the sauce. "Honestly, Sylvia, I play tug-of-war with elephants on a daily basis. It's just that I learned a long time ago that you have to have the guts and the strength of will to fight that reality, that dark side, or it'll roll right over the top of you and you'll never get out from under it." She wiped her hands on the camp T-shirt she'd thrown on as a cover-up. "Maybe David let the dark side roll over the top of him. Maybe he can't get out from under it without a helping hand. Maybe he needs someone like me to help him win his tug-of-war with the elephants." She pointed a finger in Sylvia's face, daring her to argue. "I don't think David needs to be left alone to fight his dragons. I think he needs somebody to stand beside him to help light the way, so that he can see that his dragons aren't as big as he's imagined. I intend to be his lady of light whether he likes it or not."

She looked around the camp, satisfied that everybody had something to eat. Now it was time to nourish her own hunger, and David's. "Well?" she demanded of the psychologist. "Aren't you going to say anything?"

Sylvia licked the mustard from her fingers that held a foot-long hot dog. "Good dress rehearsal. I hope you do as well in front of the audience it was intended for. Why don't you have something to eat first, though? A tug-of-war with elephants, or stubborn mules, requires energy."

There was a certain logic to that. And, too, this

conversation with David required privacy. And David still had Nick to contend with.

"Aunt Angela, will you come and sing songs and tell stories by the fire with us?" Liz drew her away from her intended meal and toward the crackling fire. Angela realized that it was only to be expected that she'd be in charge of stories. Still, it was hard to keep her mind on the details of a dozen fairy tales and keep an eagle eye out for David too.

A baker's dozen of stories and several sing-alongs later, Nick showed up, miraculously transformed back into his easygoing self. But David wasn't with him. Interrogating the still-wet pond guppy didn't help either. As far as Nick knew, David was still at the pond.

At *this* time of night? Angela helped pass out brownies and popcorn balls to everyone interested in gumming up their teeth. Surely David wouldn't have gone back into the pond alone? And if he had, since he'd admitted he hadn't been swimming in a year, could he be in trouble?

"Now, don't panic," she told herself as she tucked children into sleeping bags and closed tent flaps. "He has to be here somewhere." She walked back through camp just to make sure she hadn't missed him.

"Have you seen David yet?" Sylvia asked on her way to the makeshift shower, a robe and slippers in her hand.

Now she was going to think about panicking. "No. But I'll check in his tent. He probably snuck in and hid while I was leading the troops in the twenty-seventh chorus of 'Home on the Range.' Did you need him for something?"

"Nope. Just wanted to tell him good night. He's

a big boy." She read Angela's look. "He doesn't need to check in."

Angela made a quick tour of the camp again before checking his tent. He wasn't inside, but when she looked down there was a recently emptied dinner gray on the tent floor, a crumbled biscuit all that was left of his dinner.

"*Now* you can panic," she muttered aloud. David had obviously come back for dinner, though when he could have done so she wasn't sure. And then he'd gone back to swim alone, because there wasn't anything wet sopping up his sleeping bag or dripping on the floor. He'd gone back to the pond, and he'd gone back alone and he was probably out there right now. The water would have cooled some by now. And though it wasn't a big pond, there *were* some places where you couldn't touch bottom, and he'd said he was out of shape for swimming. Ponds being what they were, he wouldn't be able to see the bottom anywhere. He could be out there *drowning*, and no one would know!

She moved into action, already having made the decision to go and find him. There were stars out, but no moon tonight. Would he even be able to see where the shore was or tell how far away it was? And what was she doing standing around here? Grabbing a lantern, she lit it on the run and raced down the trail to the pond.

"Stupid, stupid mud!" She careened sideways into a clump of sage as she hit the trickling stream that fed the pond. "Stupid, idiotic, macho knight! If he isn't drowned, I'm going to wring his stupid neck!" She held back a sob of panic as she slid down the muddy incline. "I didn't mean it. I didn't mean it." She sent the apology heavenward. Holding her fear in check, she slid her way toward the pond with all the finesse of a baseball player sliding into home plate, the lantern held high to keep it alight.

"David?" She called out for him as she hit bottom and sank up to *her* bottom in pond muck. "David, where are you?"

An amused voice and a throaty chuckle emanated from the water's edge only a few feet away from her. "Over here, Lady Liberty. If you're looking for me, I'm over here. If you're looking for huddled masses yearning to breathe free, though, I think you've missed your turn and come to the wrong shore."

He sounded normally, disgustingly fine. Worse. He sounded ready to laugh. "Ooooohhhhhh." She plunked the lantern down so hard that the draft put it out. "Damn."

"I think you have a problem, Lady Liberty." David splashed close to her but didn't get out of the water. "I think your eternal torch went kaput."

"Will you stop calling me that?" She wiped the mud off her arms and smeared it on her face in the process. "I'm *not* Lady Liberty!" As his lady of light she wasn't doing so hot either. "And it's not a torch. It's a lantern that I brought with me because I was convinced you'd been stupid enough to go swimming alone, and I was afraid I'd need it to find your body!" She was shaking and crying and not in a mood to drag elephants anywhere.

"Angel, I didn't mean to frighten you." He splashed a bit closer, his voice tinged with apology and no little wonder. "I didn't think you'd worry. It didn't occur to me that you'd care where I was."

"You didn't realize I'd care?" Were all men this

obtuse, or was it just white knights who weren't in touch with themselves enough to know that they were white knights? "And you accuse me of having my head in the clouds? Ooooohhhhh!!" She was inarticulately fuming again. "I could drown you myself. In fact, I think I will." She struggled to get to her feet. "At the very least, you need to soak your head!" Standing up in the mud, she removed first one slimy shoe and then the other. The mucky shirt followed, along with her socks, all tossed onto the moss which she'd missed in her hasty flight down.

"Angela, what are you doing?" David backed away from the shore. "I was only kidding around earlier about the skinny-dipping."

The sound of the zipper on her pants being undone was her only reply.

He closed his eyes for a brief second. "Angela, I'm serious." He wasn't ready to share the intimacy of being naked with her yet. Lecturing Nick to have courage was one thing; having it himself was quite another. He wasn't emotionally prepared. He wasn't—

She was. She was coming into the water. "You shouldn't issue invitations if you aren't willing to live up to them."

"Now, you listen here." He wasn't going to stand, even on one foot, for that. "I can live up to any invitation I issue." His breathing quickened as she floated out to meet him. "It's only that . . ." That what? That he had enough trouble handling the woman when she was fully clothed, and he was on both feet, standing a head taller than she was. What was he supposed to do with her when she was naked and they weren't on equal footing?

She reached out to put her hands on his waist,

using him as an anchor as she tread water beside him.

He *wasn't* ready for this.

"I want you to know that I don't throw half my clothes off and hop into strange ponds with just anybody." She moved in closer, but just a little.

He moved his legs in wide circles as he swam to keep them away from hers. "I don't appreciate being used as a guinea pig for your experi—"

Angela grabbed a big handful of his hair and dunked his head under the water before he could finish the insult.

He came up sputtering under her still bra-clad breasts. "I don't need your pity, Ms. Newman." He coughed on a mouth full of water.

She shoved him under the surface again before he could stop her. You could drag an elephant to water, she thought, but it took even more effort to make him drink.

He surfaced and grabbed her hands to his chest before she could dunk him again. "What the hell are you doing?"

She smiled to herself. It was a beginning. "Trying to win a tug-of-war with an elephant." Freeing one hand, she unfastened her bra.

"Huh?" He wasn't sure any longer just which of them was living in a fantasy world.

"I was trying to tell you that it's just as scary for me to have a relationship with a man like you— cynical, pragmatic, untouchable person that you are—as it is for you to have a relationship with a woman like me." She curled her fingers in his chest hair. It felt as heavenly as she thought it would, all wet and heavy and curling, like so many dark, silky rings around her fingers. "There have been men in my life before, but none like you. You're all cold, hard facts and reasonable logic."

"And you're all idealistic optimism when there's no hope. You're a believer in fantasy in the midst of destruction." His heart pounded harder as she caressed his chest, and he couldn't move away as she slid her hips closer to his. "A fantasy," he murmured. She was that. In the darkness he could almost let himself believe in fantasies. If only fantasies weren't so much like dreams, inclined to fade away in the harsh light of day.

"I'm real," she said softly as she half floated and half clung to him in the water. "I'm here. You can touch me and see for yourself."

If only he could. "I'm not some white knight in shining armor," he said firmly. "And wishing I was won't make it so."

Angela pulled them closer to shore until they both had their feet firmly planted on the ground. She wanted to get this right and she wanted him to believe it. "A part of you is; the part that held me all night and wrapped me up in your blue robe; the part I saw with Benjy; the part that did what had to be done for Nick even though it scared him to death. That part is. I know there's another side to you, too, but that's all right." She slid out of the water and sat down on the moss, tossing her bra down like a gauntlet. "The only things I know that are all white are marshmallows and angels. Neither of them are very interesting, fulfilling, or substantial."

"Oh, no?" Why was he having so much trouble breathing? Her breasts gleamed in the starlight, the cold water dripping from her nipples, stiffening them. "I beg to differ. I can think of one angel who couldn't be more substantial, interesting, or fulfilling." He swallowed the boulder-size lump that was determined to remain lodged in his throat, and tried somewhat unsuccessfully to keep his manhood at a proper downturned angle.

"Haven't you figured that one out yet?" She laughed softly and slithered out of her panties, a naked Eve with enticing intentions. "I'm no more all angel than you are all white knight. Like you said, I'm a little angel, a little Pollyanna. But I'm part enchantress and part Pandora, too, and part *cold*." Dammit! She wasn't used to seduction, either on the giving or the receiving end. "David, are you going to come out of that pond and keep me warm?" She moved his prosthesis to a spot sure to stay dry and out of the way. It wasn't needed now. "Or are you going to make me flaunt my vulnerabilities while you hide yours? Surely a true knight in armor would have more courage."

He moved closer in to shore, the water slipping lower and lower until he was covered only up to his hips. "If we're getting literal, it's more like steel, plastic, and fiberglass, but I suppose it is more poetic the other way." He felt the weight of several of her elephants lift from his shoulders. It hadn't been that bad to joke about it. "But that's not the vulnerability I'm trying to hide." He looked down.

"Haven't you been listening?" she said teasingly. "That's what I've been trying to tell you. I don't want you to hide anything from me." Her lips twitched as he slipped from the water to sit beside her on the mossy part of the shore. "Certainly not something as bi—" The rest of her description dissolved into muffled giggles and small, slurping sounds of delight as he brought his mouth down onto hers.

"Angel, do you believe in love at first sight?" he asked when at last they both needed to come up for air.

"Yes." She said it unequivocally.

"I don't." He held her far enough away to allow some rationality to come between them. "And as much as part of me, probably the black knight part, along with . . . ah . . . other parts, would like to hide my vulnerabilities somewhere other than the pond, I can't lie to you. It would be unprofessional and unethical and just plain unfair." He kissed the tip of her nose and called himself seven kinds of a fool. How many times did anyone in his right mind turn down the chance to make love to a genuine angel? "I have grave doubts that I'd be good for you. I'm too . . ." He was too scared, that's what he was, too scared to admit to either of them that she was the best thing to come into his life since everything else had gone out of it. He was too scared of loving and losing to risk loving again.

"You're too pessimistic," she said brightly. "I'm sure we've already established that. But take heart." She leaned close enough to him that her soft breasts touched his chest. "I specialize in miracles, and I've got all night to work on you."

Six

"Angel, when I agreed that we could talk, I didn't agree that it was going to be tonight. Don't you *ever* take no for an answer?" David whispered as they snuck back into camp.

"Rarely." Angela laughed softly. "Maybe once when I was six. Anyway, tonight I'm not an angel. You're terrible with details, do you know that? Tonight I'm Pandora, and Pandora *never* takes no for an answer."

"Whoever you are, you're schizophrenic." His eyes narrowed as she bent over at the waist to pick up a fallen sock. He was doing his best not to think about the fact that all that stood between him and heaven were two scraps of underwear and his good intentions. She wasn't making it easy.

He ushered her as quietly as possible into his tent, tied the flaps closed with unceremonious haste, and lighted the Coleman lamp. "I wish you had put your clothes on before we left the pond." He snatched her other sock in from under the tent door. "Do you realize how much trouble we could get into if anybody found us together in here like this?"

"As much trouble as we could get into if nobody finds us in here together like this?"

He groaned and threw her a dry towel from his pack. He'd put his pants, socks, and shoes on by the pond. She, on the other hand, had refused to redress in her muddy clothes even for the time it took to get to camp. And she'd rationalized it all by saying that her underwear didn't reveal as much as the bikini had, and besides, everyone else but they were asleep. What kind of logic was that? David asked himself.

"If you're going to pout, I could go in search of four pairs of long overalls." She fumbled with his tent ties.

He grabbed her hands. "And have someone see you coming from my tent like that?" It *was* a good excuse to keep her with him.

"I have to go out sometime," she said in a tone of sweet reason.

"Angela, I like my job," he warned her. "I really do."

"Tell you what, I can dig a tunnel from your tent to mine. Shouldn't take more than a day or so. You're going to have to go out for food, though, in the meantime. I'm starving." She gave his tent the once-over. "You wouldn't happen to have anything to eat in here, would you?"

If he didn't, he wouldn't put it past her to traipse about out there until she found something. And she'd be out of reach then. "I might be able to scrounge up a candy bar." He crawled over the top of his sleeping bag to reach his backpack.

"Candy bar?" She followed him.

It was a small tent, an even smaller sleeping bag, and when he turned to give her the bar of white chocolate, the space was reduced to almost nothing. "Are you doing this on purpose?" he whispered into her neck.

"What on purpose?" She smiled innocently into his thick hair.

"Pandora, didn't anyone tell you that people who play with fire get burned?"

"I wish there *was* something burning in here." She finished the candy, handed David the wrapper, and crossed her arms over her shoulders. "It's freezing in this place. You don't mind if I get into your sleeping bag to keep warm while we talk, do you?" she asked as she crawled inside. "Aren't you cold?"

"Cold?" It was a foreign word, without meaning. She had to be kidding. He wiped his face with a perspiring hand.

"Here." She held the sleeping bag open. "Why don't you take all those wet things off and get in. I'll even close my eyes and count to twenty if that'll help."

"I must be out of my mind," he muttered as he threw his clothes off and got in next to her before she got to ten. "Aren't I supposed to close my eyes now?" he asked as she began removing her bra and panties for a second time in one evening. Just how much willpower was he supposed to have?

"No. I can do it under the covers."

So could he. Under the covers. Above the covers. Outside on the tent. Under the trees. Just *anywhere*. And the feel of her squirming out of her clothes was even more erotic than watching her do it had been. And that had nearly driven him out of his mind.

"Angel . . ." He moaned as her breasts brushed against him. "One of my legs may be partly constructed of steel from the shin down. But I assure you that the rest of me from the shin up isn't. The rest of me is flesh and bone and blood, hot blood, and—"

"And I thought you wanted to talk." Angela snuggled against him.

"Talk? No. You wanted to talk. I wanted to sleep." Then. Now he wanted to do neither, the proof of which was pressing eagerly into the side of her thigh. That much had to be obvious even to someone with her head in the clouds.

"Okay." She yawned and watched him out of the corner of her eye. "We can sleep now and talk in the morning. G'night." Closing both eyes she rolled over on one side and pressed her naked behind against the front of him.

Maybe she was right. Maybe he was made of steel. It was beginning to feel like it. "Angela, I've changed my mind. I don't want to sleep."

"Would it help if I kept my eyes closed, my mouth shut, and you pretended to be talking in your sleep?" The muffled question came from his pillow.

"I don't want to talk either."

"Actually, at the moment neither do I." She rolled back over and fit herself perfectly into his arms. "But don't you think we should get all of that out of the way before we get down to the fun stuff?"

She wasn't going to give up, was she? "What do you want to talk about?"

"Lots of things." She drew tiny, loving patterns on his bare chest with her fingers. "But, for the sake of saving time, right now all I want to know is when and how you lost your leg, and why Sylvia seems to think you got hurt, more than physically, when it happened."

"In a nutshell?" Somehow the past didn't hurt so much when the present, especially his present company, felt so good. "I was engaged when I found out I had bone cancer. She was like a beautiful, story-book princess, all innocence and naïveté. We were in the middle of plans for a huge wedding when they told me I had to go into the hospital. Before then, she was always the fragile one, the one I protected from life's problems and unpleasantness. Maybe I was like a knight in shining armor then." He shrugged as the memories washed over him, unaware just then that the woman who was now holding him in her arms wasn't that kind of fragile. "In the space of a few days everything changed." He drew his legs up, unconsciously putting the whole one out in front so that if she touched him, she wouldn't feel the loss that he was remembering. "I lost my foot, my shin, then my lifestyle, most of my friends, and then her. Finally I lost even myself. Boom, boom, boom. It's taken a year to get back in touch with my emotions again. There are people like Sylvia who don't think I've completely found myself yet."

"We could make a start in that direction tonight." Angela used her feet and toes to explore the rough hair on his muscular right calf, not stopping when she reached its end. "I'm not some shallow cream puff of a woman who's going to faint to learn that her white knight has some rough edges." She clenched her toes around a patch of his leg hair and pulled until he yelped softly. "I'm a woman who just happens to look on the bright side of reality. And in any case, I'm different from her. I lov—" Love? Had that been what she'd been about to say? The realization hit her full force and with such intensity that she stopped her argument mid-sentence. She was in love with David Ortega; with the psychologist as well as the man he was underneath; with both black and white knight sides of him; with the plastic and steel as much as the flesh and blood. It was all the same. It was all him. But how to convince him of that when all his trust and love was hidden behind emotional armor stronger than any steel?

"You what?" he prompted.

"I was about to say that I could lust after your body at lot more easily if we stopped talking and engaged our mouths in something other than speech." She teasingly let him see the part of her feelings she thought he might be able to accept. Whether he trusted her heart or not, there was no way he could deny that her nipples were stiff with desire for him, or that his thigh was warm and moist from where she'd had her inner thighs wrapped around it. He had to know that she wanted him.

"Angel, I don't need sex therapy." His voice was tight. "And, as I told you before, I'm not interested in your pity."

"How very convenient." She cuddled closer to him, taking supreme feminine delight in his quick physical response to her. "I'm not interested in pity from you either."

"You can't kiss frogs in real life and have them turn into Prince Charmings."

"I don't want to kiss a frog." She wrinkled her nose in mock disgust. "I want to kiss you. Besides, do you know what frogs *do* when you try to kiss them?" She made another horrible face. "In any case, I don't want a Prince Charming. I want you." It was the truth. She did want him—with or without armor. "I want my knight in shining armor. You're it."

"Damn it all, Angel." He was finding it harder and harder to think with her nibbling seductively on his lips. "My armor, such as it is, is over there along with my socks and shoes. I'm no knight. Moreover, I can't slay dragons. Believing I can is only going to open us both up to a lot of pain." He kissed her hand impulsively as she drew her fingers across his lips, all the while wondering at his sanity. "My ex-fiancée thought I was some kind of an invincible superman too. I couldn't live up to that image for her, and I'm never, ever going to try to again, not even for you." He couldn't go through that hell again. Far better to set his sights low and be happily surprised. Far, far better never to dream than to soar as high as he could with this woman and then crash to earth from five miles up. "It doesn't take a trained psychologist to see that a man like me doesn't belong with a believer in fairy tales. Why can't you see that?" She couldn't because she had her eyes closed and her face pressed into his neck. He could feel her there, the sensation traveling all the way down to his toes.

Angela murmured something reassuring and kissed his Adam's apple, following it with her lips as it bobbed up and down in his throat. It wasn't the time for logic. Love wasn't necessarily logical.

He closed his eyes, resolving to stop all this nonsense just as soon as he could form a coherent sentence. Just at the moment his vocal cords were too excited to do more than vibrate helplessly. Where, oh where were his professional calm and his eloquence? "Angela, you aren't listening to a thing I'm saying," he said finally, his voice a mere croak.

"That's because you're not saying a thing worth listening to. Now, take me, for instance." Please, she begged him silently. "I'm saying some very important things."

"Mmmmm?" He was losing control fast.

She kissed the hollow at the base of his throat, using her lips to gauge his rapidly increasing pulse. "I'm trying to communicate with you, to put it in your blasted psychologist's jargon, via body language." She intertwined her fingers with his and held his arms apart so that they couldn't prevent her from kissing a direct line from his neck to his heart. "Why aren't you listening?"

"I guess because I was too busy telling you why we couldn't—" He broke off, moaning in defeat, refusing to listen any longer to either his conscious or subconscious fears.

"The only thing I can think of that we *can't* do," Angela said, "is play footsies with four feet and twenty toes." She licked her lips to taste the warm muskiness of his chest, and winding around him, brought one of their clasped hands to her breasts. "Do you really want to play footsies with four feet and twenty toes when you could be playing with . . ." Her words drifted off as his fingers touched and circled the nipple of one breast, bringing it and its envious counterpart to instant attention.

Had she been about to make a point? Did it matter? Her lips formed an "O" of pleasure as he freed both hands from her grasp and brought them in to caress her body. Her skin seemed to grow a multitude of new nerve endings just for him, all of them designed to transmit the pleasure of his touch directly to her brain. After the months she'd spent feeling physically and emotionally numb because of Liz, this was like being drunk on ambrosia from the gods. And he had to be feeling it as much as she was. Gathering him close with arms strong and determined to keep him there, she stared into his face for the answer.

"David? David, are you in there?" She wrinkled her brow curiously. The man who stared so intently back into her eyes was not the same man she'd locked horns with a few days ago. He wasn't even the same man whom she'd been trying to convince to make love with her a few minutes ago. Like the difference between a real man and a doppelgänger, this David was consumed by a passionate intensity that transcended his fears. She could see it in his face and feel it in his hands as they moved over her. There was no hesitation in him now, no uncertainty, only a burning, not-to-be-denied desire. She'd seen a glimpse of it, and she'd felt a spark of it, on that first day. The spark grew into a raging wildfire now, too big for even him to keep under his iron control.

"Pandora, this knight needs more than castles in the air and a lady's chaste favor. If you're looking for a brotherly, romantic kind of love, for a chivalrous—"

"If I was looking for chivalrous, I'd read some of my own fairy tales." She smiled wickedly at him. "And, in case you haven't stopped talking long enough to notice, I'm not looking for a book." She spread her hands out over his chest and followed the contours of his body downward. "And I'm not looking for a book mark." She reached his stomach and curled her fingers in some of the hair that led to his groin. She stretched her hands out tentatively to encircle him, a wave of uncertainty making her hands tremble. Did he want her as much as she wanted him, or had her hopeful imagination wished for too much?

With a garbled half plea, half moan he answered her question, reaching down to hold and move her hand against him in a less hesitant manner. It drove any thought of conversation from both their minds.

Nothing, absolutely nothing had ever felt this good or this right, Angela realized. Nothing she'd ever experienced had ever prepared her for what it felt like to have him moving over her body. She felt bereft when he pulled away from her to extricate them from the sleeping bag. The sensation of loss didn't last for long, replaced almost instantly with sensations of another variety. She arched her back as he cupped both of her breasts in his hands and brought them to full, aching arousal with his fingertips and mouth. And just when she thought that there was no greater pleasure than the feel of his wet lips and tongue suckling her breasts, his hands dropped lower and gently parted her legs. Lying in a force field of contentment, she couldn't have moved if she wanted to. She didn't want to. Starting out in slow, seeking circles, he moved his fingers from her inner thighs in to the outer edges of her moist femininity and then beyond, stroking and teasing in an ever increasing rhythm until her body was as taut as a bowstring and shaking with her need of him. As the avalanche of sensation hit and carried her away, she reached for him to guide him into her, wanting him, needing him as she would the very oxygen she breathed. His was the hard life's essence that her softness craved, the final completion she needed to finish the ascent into heaven. Holding the tip of him next to her flesh, she pressed him down toward their final destination.

And she didn't understand what in the world

happened when he covered her mouth with one hand and held her impatient fingers with the other. Her eyes were seeing him alone. Her ears were in tune to the music they were making. The outside world didn't exist.

Except that it did, in reality, and he was more in tune with that than she was.

"David? David? David? David, are you in there?" Sylvia's voice was muffled, but there was no mistaking the sharpness of her tone or the urgency of her message. "I need you to help me find Angela Newman."

"Angela?" David's own passion-glazed eyes cleared and he shook his head just as if he had been asleep as Sylvia assumed. "What for?"

"It's Liz." Sylvia called low-toned instructions out to others outside the tent. "We need to find Angela because Liz is having some problems with her medication and we're going to have to take her back down the mountain to camp."

The temperature in the tent felt like it had fallen fifty degrees in an instant, bathing Angela in icy chills.

"I'll get her and bring her right there," David barked to Sylvia and threw the sleeping bag and its lingering intimacy aside. "Did you radio the hospital that we'll be coming in?"

"Just a few minutes ago," Sylvia said. "And they're sending up another couple of supervisors to take the rest of the kids back down in the morning as usual. I thought you might like to go down with Angela and Liz on this run."

Were his feelings for Angela that obvious? He didn't have the time to think about that now or how it made him feel. He had to get dressed and see to it that Angela was ready to go when Liz was. Angela. He looked at the woman at his side. Caught in a terror even her cheerful idealism couldn't deal with, she was still sitting, huddled in his sleeping bag.

A paralyzing fear and an equally heavy blanket of guilt had settled over her like a fog. What could she have been thinking of? What had possessed her to cavort around as though she hadn't a care in the world when Liz needed her? Had the little girl been calling for her? Had they been looking for her in her tent? And how was she going to forgive herself if something happened to Liz while she got herself together, got dressed, and got out there?

"Angela, come on. Snap out of it." David shook her gently, his hand firm and strong on her shoulder. "You can't do Liz any good sitting here feeling guilty."

She looked up at him, wondering how he knew what she was feeling.

"I've come to accept that people live or not no matter how many night-long vigils you stand by their beds," he said gently. "You can't change things from being what they *are* or from what they *will be*, not even if you sit up around the clock wishing you could change things. Now, come on. We've got to hurry." Thrusting a pile of clothes in her hand, he went in search of his own apparel.

Hurry! The word and the reason behind it sank in then, spurring her into furious action, filling her system with adrenaline. Her knight cum psychologist was faster, already donning both his physical and emotional armor. When he was finished, he looked ready to fight whatever dragon was awaiting outside.

"I'll meet you outside," she promised as he exited

the tent. "I just have to run to my tent and get into some dry clothes."

"As long as you're ready when we're ready to transport her." He was out the tent on the run, already having forgotten that he'd even been to a fantasy world with her, or even that one existed.

How long did it take to find clean socks and underwear in a pack, and to put them and a shirt and pants on, right side out, in the dark, with overly nervous, clumsy fingers? Angela tried counting the minutes, a second at a time, to herself as she dressed. One thousand one, one thousand two, one thousand three . . . But it seemed to slow her down, and she kept forgetting where she was anyway, or how many minutes she'd already used up. When she emerged from the tent, her own this time, it was with her shoes in hand, her shirt collar tucked inside, the buttons done up unevenly, and her hair in a wild disarray.

"Hiya, baby, how're you doing?" She knelt beside Liz just as two nurses were finishing with her pulse and blood pressure measurements.

"I feel dizzy, and I'm hot and it feels heavy when I try to breathe." Liz took hold of Angela's hand and refused to let go, even when they lifted her up to put her into the back of a waiting Jeep.

"I'll hold her." Angela's voice was icy with determination as she climbed up into the Jeep and held out her arms.

"But the rules—" The driver looked doubtful.

"Can be broken this one time." David climbed in beside her. "I'll take the responsibility."

Angela turned to thank him but stopped as she saw the look on his face and in his eyes. Both were cold and unreadable, without even a hint of warmth. And she had a terrible feeling that when he did, if he did, display any emotion, it would be that sort of generic, canned sympathy that all Liz's doctors and counselors used when telling her that there was no hope. David wasn't going the extra mile and letting her ride with Liz to the hospital out of any special feeling he had for her. He was letting her because it was his professional way of helping her face and accept what he saw as inevitable. He was granting her, as he would have to anyone else, some private time to say good-bye! She squelched the sudden flare of anger and turned her full attention back to Liz, not willing to waste any precious time or effort to change his mind. Just at the moment she wasn't sure why she'd wasted as much as she had. How could she be in love with a man who steadfastly refused to believe that Liz would live? How could she see him as a white knight, as any kind of a knight at all, if he wouldn't even lift a sword to fight the dragon, if he went into battle thinking that the dragon had already won? She willed away a sudden gush of tears along with the doubts that had brought them on. She did love him, but that didn't mean he was always right. And she couldn't allow herself to think that he might be. The little girl who was curled up in a down sleeping bag, dozing on her lap, didn't need anyone else doubting her ability to live. She needed someone who believed in miracles. She needed someone to banish the dragons.

And perhaps a roomful of guardian angels couldn't do that. But if Liz thought they could, then maybe that belief would give her the strength and courage to fight just a little harder, for just a little longer. And maybe that extra effort would be just enough to turn the tide. It was a big maybe.

But then, Angela had seen maybes work before. And in any case, since she couldn't count on anything else for sure, a maybe was far better than nothing. She waited until Liz had been installed in a hospital room before taking off to find the art supplies she would need.

When she made it back, the doctors had already come and gone, and David was just on his way out the door.

"What are you doing?" He looked down at the box of poster paints and at the stack of two- by three-foot construction paper she carried. "I thought you'd gone back to Liz's cabin to get some sleep."

"I couldn't sleep over there when Liz is here." She set the supplies out on a table that Liz shared with the room's only other occupant, Benjy. Both children were sound asleep. "Besides, when I found out that they were putting Liz in with Benjy, I remembered Benjy's guardian angel, and it gave me an idea."

"I think it would be a better idea for you to decide to get some sleep." David rubbed a weary hand over his own tired face. "The doctors have done everything they can for her now."

"I know." She opened a quart tub of bright yellow poster paint and set it within easy reach of her construction-paper canvas. "Now it's my turn."

"Angela, you can't spend the night here." How was he supposed to deal with an otherwise bright, well-educated woman who believed that paper angels could help a child overcome cancer? He warred with himself over whether to help her accept Liz's probable fate, or to let her go on believing in the impossible just so she would stop looking at him with those hurt, accusing eyes. "For one thing, it might wake Benjy." It was an excuse, but perhaps it would convince her to let go of her search for a miracle at least long enough to rest.

"I'm not going to wake Benjy, and you know it," she said softly as she started to paint an angel. "In the first place, I paint quietly. In the second, you know as well as I do that Benjy prefers to sleep with all the lights blazing and, if possible, a radio blaring away. And third, the reason they put Liz and Benjy together is so that the nurses don't have to wake up everybody else in the hospital every time they do hourly checks on these two. I'm not going to disturb either one of them as much as the nurses when they come in every hour. And in any case, I'm not going." She stopped painting angel's wings long enough to see whether she'd won or lost the battle. The man she had almost made love to was gone, banished to wherever he'd sent his hopes and dreams. The man who had replaced him was the same objective clinical psychologist who had tried to get rid of her that first day. Perhaps he'd come to realize that she wasn't so easily gotten rid of.

She hardened herself to the pain as he turned and strode wordlessly out the door, unaware that there was an anguish in his heart to match her own.

Seven

"Hey, lady! Be careful or you're going to step on my puppy!"

Angela froze in mid-step and tried to juggle the construction-paper leaning tower of Pisa she carried in her arms.

"See?" The same small, little-boy voice called out to her again from somewhere under the art supplies. "He's right here under your foot. If you move, you'll smash his head for sure!"

Angela gripped the bags in her arms tighter and balanced on one foot. "Can you rescue him, please?" she called to the as yet unseen child. She'd been up all night making a host of angels. She hadn't slept. She hadn't eaten. She hadn't had her first cup of morning coffee. She had, in fact, only left camp in order to purchase more art supplies. It wasn't the morning to play hopscotch with living, breathing, easily smashed targets when she counted herself lucky to be able to put one foot in front of the other without tripping herself. She didn't need the added challenge of an obstacle course.

"I'll get him, lady." A small blond head peeked at her through several boxes of crayons and tubes of paint. "You just hold still."

That was easier said than done. She teetered precariously as a warm, fuzzy body burrowed in between her ankles and tiny claws scratched at her pants. Her balance deteriorated even further as the owner of that fuzzy ball of fur did a nose dive after his pet. She was able to stay on her feet until his series of coaxing whistles brought the rest of the roly-poly litter out of their box on the run.

"Oh, my heavens!" Reeling drunkenly this way and that, she somehow managed to dance a jig around the puppies and their keeper before landing ignominiously on her backside directly in front of the store. Papers, puppies, and people littered the sidewalk along with her scattered art supplies.

"Miss? Are you all right? Did you get hurt?" The manager of the store where she'd bought the supplies hauled her to her feet, throwing a look of severe warning in the direction of the miniature zookeeper at his side. "Did this young man cause you to fall?"

Angela glanced down at the child whose large eyes silently petitioned her to keep silent. Even the puppies looked subdued, all of them cowed into a huddle around their young master's legs. "This young man?" She looked the store manager squarely in the eye. "On the contrary. This young man very politely offered to help pick up my packages when I slipped. It's my fault, really. I shouldn't have tried to carry so much at one time."

"Well . . ." The man shrugged in relief, glad at least that he wasn't facing doctor bills or a lawsuit. "If you're sure you're all right, I'll just help you with your purchases and see that you get safely to your car."

The puppy baron intervened. "No. I'll do that. I was going to anyway." He waited until the manager had gone back inside before turning a friendly face up to his benefactress. "Thanks for helping me out of trouble. I'd have gotten in *big* trouble if I'd made you fall down and you told him about it. You wouldn't want to help me out of some more trouble and buy one of my puppies, would ya?" He watched her with hopeful blue eyes while one of the proposed purchases gnawed on her purse.

"You've got to be kidding." She wiggled her fingers and toes, grateful she hadn't bruised anything more than her dignity.

"Nope." He shook his head sorrowfully and began putting his charges back into the too-small cardboard box they'd just climbed out of. "My dad says I gotta get rid of all of 'em today or the lady who rents us the apartment is gonna get rid of all of 'em tomorrow. And you know what *that* means."

Angela stooped to retrieve her packages, shaking one fat puppy off a bag, only to have another take his place. "You don't mean . . . Surely he didn't mean that? Who could do that to a puppy?"

"Yeah." His mouth turned down at the corners and he drew one chubby finger across his throat, making a sickeningly ominous sound as he did so. "But I don't want to say it 'cause I don't want 'em to know."

Angela looked down at the puppies again and back to the boy. "You're sure about this?" Maybe he was making it up?

"Real sure." He nodded morosely. "I heard her say it. Me 'n' these puppies were behind the door when she told my dad he was lucky she was letting me stay, as much trouble as I was." He lifted one of the innocent-looking balls of drooling fur up for her to get a closer look. "I think she'll let me slide, but these guys gotta go."

There was a sucker born every minute, Angela thought even as she spoke. "What kind are they?" She knelt beside the box in spite of her best intentions. She was too tired to be strong today.

He shrugged, then stroked one of the soft heads. "I dunno. My mom said their mother was the friendly type, and their dad the obliging sort. But I dunno what that makes the babies. Maybe they're the obliging, soft, friendly kind?" He picked one of them up and buried his face in its furry back. "I know they're the kind that likes to follow you around a lot and then sleep on your pillow at night."

"Oh." She put her hand out in the box to see which one of the puppies liked her. She was mobbed by all four pink licking tongues. "That kind." She was going to regret this, if not now, then surely as soon as David got wind of it. "How much are you asking for one of them?"

"Maybe a dollar fifty?" He looked hopeful. "And for that I'll even help pick up all your stuff." He went about the chore as if she'd already paid him for his trouble and taken the puppy off his hands. "See, I don't really make any money off them. You saw that store manager. He's real mean. And he won't let me hang around here unless I go in and buy something every once in a while. They have ice-cream cones here for only fifty cents a scoop." He put two more escapees back in their box in resignation. "I figure it's gonna take me another coupla hours, and maybe six cones, to get rid of all these guys, because everybody I ask already has a dog. Do you have a dog?"

"I guess I do now." She opened her purse for the money. "Actually, your puppy wouldn't be for me. I have a niece who is very ill and in the hospital. I think a puppy might be just the thing to cheer her up, maybe give her the motivation to get well." It might help even more than another angel. "I'm not sure how the people at the hospital are going to like having a puppy around, though." Who was she kidding? Even now she could hear David's head hitting the roof. "So maybe you could pick out a nice, quiet one?"

All four remaining puppies yipped and yapped in excitement as he whooped for joy. There wasn't a quiet one in the bunch.

"That's hard." He snapped the wad of bubble gum in his mouth as he thought. "I don't have a real quiet one. I have a *small* one. Maybe he'd make a smaller noise than the others. But if I can only save one from you know"—he made the ominous motion across his neck again and rolled his eyes in her direction—"then you might want to save the prettiest one. Or there's my favorite, the ugliest one. Maybe you should take that one because nobody else would want him. And then there's the one who eats shoes. He's not going to go over very big either." He bit his lower lip and looked at her worriedly. "Maybe I shouldn't have told you about that one," he said as he thrust the box toward her. "Here. You decide which one's gonna be here tomorrow and which ones aren't."

The kid had a future as a Washington lobbyist, she thought. He knew just which buttons to push. She extracted six dollars from her purse and tried to find the bright side of this situation.

"Are you gonna take all of 'em?" The little boy gaped at her in awe. "You mean you're gonna make sure *all* of 'em live?"

"*All* of them," she promised with a seriousness that he wouldn't begin to understand. "After all, what could they do to me for bringing four puppies into a hospital that they wouldn't do for just one?"

"You're a real nice lady," he said sincerely.

"I may have to ask you for a personal reference later," she commented dryly. "For now, though, why don't you help me load the puppies into my car. It's right over there."

"No problem, lady." Dragging the box full of puppies over to the car, he picked them all up in his arms for a good-bye hug.

"No problem," she muttered. "How do I get myself into situations like this?" David was going to have kittens over her puppies. No problem, indeed!

"I stuck a few cans of their puppy food inside." He crawled out of her back seat, stuffing the puppies back in when they tried to follow him. "Can I do anything else for you before you take 'em away?"

"Yeah." She climbed in the front seat of her sports car and sat down on the paw of one of the puppies who'd managed to squeeze around to the front. She turned a deaf ear to his shrill yelps and dropped him back into his box. Oh, this was going to be great fun. "You can tell your mom to keep the friendly kind away from the obliging sort in the future. You're not going to find too many more masochists who take pleasure in tickling the dragon's tail. I think I'm probably the last of a dying breed."

She waved good-bye to her peace of mind and the little boy, and sat in her car trying to decide what to do. Maybe she wouldn't tell David about the puppies. Maybe she'd just wait until the little blond moppet's favorite pet ate David's shoes. Of course, with her luck, David's foot would still be in the shoe.

"You can't stall all day," she told herself. "You might as well go face the music." She put the key in the ignition, turned it, and listened as the puppies made their own music, growling in shrill harmony as the engine came to life, died, caught, and died again. "This cannot happen to me." She tried the engine again, adding to the din with a whine of her own as it refused to even turn over.

It was not going to be her day, a fact that was proven out when the first person she reached when she called the camp was David. She held the phone out away from her ear and listened, sort of long distance, as he lectured her about driving a foreign-made car, about driving an improperly maintained vehicle, about driving in the first place since she'd had no sleep, and about the fact that she was driving him crazy. He didn't know the half it! Massaging her aching temples, she let him wind down, only momentarily considering hanging up on him as a lost cause. He was annoyed enough with her as it was. He'd spent most of the night after their confrontation pacing the hospital corridors like a caged tiger, his expression growing grimmer and his mood darker with each passing hour. Why he didn't simply turn his untouchable, objective self on, and turn her and her eccentricities off was something of a mystery to her. She knew that the paper angels she'd been up all night drawing and stringing from the ceiling brought him no joy. Quite the contrary. Most of them he grudgingly ducked under and around, as if they had no place in his world. The others, like her, he seemed not to see, as though they weren't real, as though she, and what she'd thought they'd had together, wasn't real either.

She wiped at a traitorous tear after he'd promised to send someone for her, returned to the car, and fondled a sympathetically whining puppy's head. Another minute and she'd have them all howling in mutual sorrow. She couldn't afford that. She had to pull herself together. Liz needed to see someone strong at her side, someone who believed in her. Which wasn't going to happen anytime soon if David forgot to send someone to come pick her up!

She got out of the car and paced back and forth in front of the gas station she'd had her car towed to. It had seemed an eternity since she'd made that call. Where *was* her ride?"

Surely it could not be the motorcycle that pulled up alongside her, or the black-leather-clad man who piloted it. The monstrous machine rumbled to a stop and a black-leather-gloved hand flipped a helmet visor open to reveal weary blue eyes and an unsmiling face.

"You do realize that my job description does *not* include rescuing damsels in distress?" David removed the leather gloves and stuffed them into his front jacket pocket.

The dragon chuckled maliciously in Angela's fatigued imagination and she backed up against the car to shield her puppies from black knights and dragons alike.

"Nobody asked you to do the rescuing," she snapped defensively. "All I asked for was a ride back to Casa de los Niños. My car has a broken whatchamacallit and they can't get the part to fix it for a few days."

"A broken whatchamacallit?" He groaned. "Never mind. Forget I asked. I don't have time to ask. I've got to get back to the camp. Hop on."

"Hop on what? Hop on *that*?" She eyed the motorcycle incredulously. He had to be hallucinating from lack of sleep. In the first place, she'd never wanted to end her own life badly enough to get on one of those things. And in the second place, there was no way four puppies were going to be able to come along. "I can't," she exclaimed emphatically.

"Can't?" He frowned at her. "Of course you can. It's easy. The camp's not that far. The roads are paved most of the way. I'm a careful driver, even more so since I have to compensate for my lost foot. And I even brought you a helmet." Leaning around, he unzipped a dark maroon daypack that was strapped to the sissy bar, and withdrew another helmet.

"Keep it." She waved the helmet away. "I'm not getting on that contraption. And I'm sorry I bothered you. I'll take a taxi back, or a bus, or I'll hitch a ride. I'll walk if I have to. But I'm not getting on that thing."

"It's not a *thing*." He got off the bike impatiently, swinging his leg over the seat to the ground. "It's a Kawasaki 750. And it doesn't go much over seventy miles per hour unless I push it, and I promise not to do that if you're on the back. How's that?"

"Not good enough." She spread her hands wide over the open window of her car and tried to think fast to prevent him from sounding off about the puppies.

"I'm in no mood for arguments today, Angel," he warned. "You aren't going to find a taxi or a bus to take you out to the camp. I won't hear of you hitching a ride. And the nearest car-rental agency is in the next town." He stopped and unbuckled his helmet as an oddly high-pitched whine sounded through its protective padding. "And you can't walk that far." He removed the helmet altogether and dropped it over the top of the sissy bar. "And what is that sound coming from your car?"

"The broken whatchamacallit?" she offered.

"I don't think so." He looked over her shoulder into the front seat where one of the puppies had escaped to.

"I don't either." Why try to avoid the unavoidable? "I think it's probably coming from the puppies."

"Oh." For a split second he seemed relieved. "For just a minute there I thought you were going to tell me you'd found a baby in a cabbage patch somewhere. That would be just like you. A puppy is much better. A puppy is—a puppy? Your puppy?" He moved her aside to get a better look.

"More like four puppies," she corrected and got them all out of the car, holding them and their small box in her arms. "And they're not mine, not exactly. I got them for Liz and Benjy and the rest of the kids in the ward. So, I suppose in a way they're part yours, as a representative of Casa de los Niños. Now all we have to do is find a way to get them back, since obviously they can't all fit on your motorcycle." She had known it wasn't going to be so simple, but—

"Oh, no." He glared at the fuzzy-headed interlopers. "No, no, no, no, no, no! This disaster is all yours, and the only thing you can do is find a way to take them back wherever you got them from."

"No dice." She hung on to the box for dear life, and tried to ignore the puppies, who were chewing on her hair and clawing at her shirt for attention. "If I return them, the little boy said they'd all wind up at the bottom of a pond somewhere in a gunnysack full of rocks."

"What little boy?"

"The one who sold them to me."

"You bought that story?" He laughed a little and then more as the full extent of her answer occurred to him. "You bought them? I'd have charged him to haul them away."

"You no doubt would have." She glared at him, then turned on her heel and started to walk away. "I, on the other hand, am at least partially human," she called over her shoulder. "I have feelings, compassion, a little sympathy."

"I have all those things too," he said, aggrieved, and following closely in her wake. "But you can't save every single puppy who's destined to have a short life."

"I can try," she retorted stubbornly. "I certainly am saving these four."

"Not at the camp, you aren't." He fell in step beside her. "The camp has a policy that strictly forbids anyone to bring a pet with him or her when they come to stay."

"I'm not bringing them to stay. I'm bringing them for a visit."

"They won't bend the rules on this one," he said in an ominously low voice. "It would make too much work for the staff."

"I'll take care of the puppies and feed them myself."

"You *can't* bring those animals to the camp." He yelled over the top of the puppies as if they had some say in the matter.

"You have horses in camp. They're animals." She stuffed a curious nose back in the box. "And I'm sure they make much bigger messes than four puppies would."

He was beginning to wonder whether it was possible to win an argument with this woman. "That's not the point. Horses are a part of the program."

"Puppies could be too. I'll bet the kids would like them, and I know I've read somewhere that pets can be therapeutic."

"It doesn't matter if the kids would like them or not. The board of directors wouldn't."

"I wonder how much it would take to change their minds?" Dear heavens, she thought, these puppies could end up costing her quite a bit more than six dollars and a whopper of a headache.

"It would be a lot easier to convince them to provide a gunnysack full of rocks and permission to use the pond." He looked around then, only vaguely aware before that they were walking away from the main part of town. "Where are you going?"

"To get them some food." She looked around for a store, and spotting a convenience store on the corner, set the puppies down on the pavement so she could get her wallet out of her pocket.

"Get them some knockout drops too." David lifted an escaping puppy back into its box with his motorcycle boot. "You'll never get them inside the main gate any other way."

"Do you know that you have all the personality of the grim reaper crossed with the Grinch who stole Christmas? You probably eat puppies for breakfast! If you had an ounce of heart, you wouldn't be trying so hard to come up with reasons why I won't be able to get them in. You'd be trying to help me." She knelt and scooped up an escapee, then thrust the box of puppies into his surprised hands. "You're drafted. Hold them until I get back, and for heaven's sake, don't hurt them."

"Don't hurt them?" he repeated as she disappeared into the store. "What does she think I am? It's not that I don't like dogs," he pointed out to a curious passerby. "I just don't see how a bunch of flea-ridden mongrels are going to help the kids get better. And I know that's what she expects. I'm trying to keep her from being bitterly disappointed," he then told the puppies as he scratched one's ear. "Why does that make me the bad guy?"

He poked a set of legs back into the box and groaned aloud. She was doing it again. Without even being aware of it she was stripping him of the only defenses he had. He couldn't afford to lose those defensive walls. He couldn't afford to believe that paper guardian angels would protect critically ill kids. He didn't want to think about a room full of puppies that in all likelihood would live far longer than the children they were supposed to comfort. Most of all, he couldn't afford to fall in love with the illusion of love and strength that Angela offered. That kind of love and untried strength lasted only until the fantasies they were based on crumpled under the weight of a harsher, stronger reality. It wasn't that he didn't want to believe, only that he didn't dare. Some things were too cripplingly painful to be endured twice.

"Well, for Pete's sake," Angela exclaimed as she scrambled to round up fugitive puppies before they made it to the busy street. "I don't see how you manage to keep such an eagle eye on a camp full of kids, when you can't manage to keep four puppies in a box." She stooped to grab the last of the wandering brood.

"I only set them down for a minute," he said. He had to get this settled before the baby-animal appeal of the puppies and his desire to please Angela swayed his better judgment. "And in case you haven't noticed, you're not doing any better."

The first two puppies she'd corralled had gotten free again, climbing on top of and over their siblings to the box's edge. Dropping one back into his cardboard jail with a thump, she made a lunge for the other and ended up with one arm around a puppy and the other around David's legs.

She looked up at him plaintively. "Are you sure you don't rescue damsels in distress?"

He latched onto the runaway by its tail. "Sir Galahad to the rescue." He was going to regret this. But not until she stopped looking at him like he'd just found the Holy Grail. "All right. All right. If I'm going to put my job on the line and help you smuggle these mongrels into camp, we'd better have more of a plan than I'm sure you've devised."

She dazzled him with a brilliant smile. Miracles *did* happen every once in a while, just often enough to renew her faith in them. "I'm the president of a publishing company," she informed him with no little pride. "I always have a plan. It's just that sometimes it's a little avant-garde."

"I'll bet your board of directors loves that," he said dryly as he hauled her to her feet. "What do you bribe them with?"

"Rising stock prices." She laughed as they carried the dogs and sack with dog food and dishes to a small grassy area adjacent to the convenience store. "That and the promise that just as soon as Janet's husband, Tom, is discharged from the service, and can be trained to take over my job, I'll quit and go back to writing full time. You see, I never wanted to be the president," she said as she opened pouches of dog food and poured them into the dishes. "It was only that Janet and I wanted to keep the major decision-making position in the family, and Janet has a terrible business sense."

"And you don't?" He dumped the puppies unceremoniously out onto the grass and stood back to watch them wriggle their ways to the food.

"Actually, I'm quite good at my job," she said seriously as she watched the puppies eat. "Contrary to the ugly rumors someone at camp has started, I cope very well with the real world. It's just that I prefer not to. Luckily for me, after I've finished training Tom, I'll be more valuable as an author-illustrator than I will as an executive, so I won't have any trouble with the board on that score. With any luck, in just a few months I'll be able to indulge in my fantasies to my heart's content and not have to worry about the L.A. office from nine to five every day. Who knows"—she said it lightly, not daring to look at him or even to hope it might be possible—"maybe I'll even find someone to share my fantasies with."

David reached down to lift a puppy off his artificial foot. Full of food, and drowsily content, the puppy seemed to have been searching for a safe haven to sleep in when it ran into the leather barrier.

"Not very comfortable, huh, sport?" David asked as he tucked the sluggish pooch into his inner jacket pocket and reached down for another refugee, making sure that his eyes never came into contact with Angela's. If they did, she would surely be able to see that he would give everything he possessed to share a fantasy with her. He would give anything in the world to share a lifetime of fantasies with her.

All he could do was play at being the gallant knight she dreamed of, rescuing puppies and damsels in distress until a real knight came along for her. Knowing that didn't make accepting it any easier. And he couldn't bring himself to answer her and say he hoped she did find someone to share her fantasies with.

"David?" She touched his jacket sleeve curiously, her expression puzzled. He'd withdrawn from her again, climbing back behind his castle walls and barricading the doors. Whatever vulnerabilities she'd inadvertently uncovered, he wasn't going to let her see.

"We have to get back." He prevented her from asking the questions that were in her eyes, using the one argument that was certain to work. "I told Liz and Benjy that I'd bring you in to see them as soon as possible. I think they want to enlist your services as a costume designer for tomorrow night's costume party." He tucked the two remaining puppies into her sweatshirt and turned back toward the motorcycle. "Maybe you could outfit them as the local dog catchers, ones with very realistic props."

"Maybe I could." Angela's expression brightened. "You know, if they're well enough to plan costumes for a party, then that must be a good sign. It must mean that the new medicine is beginning to be effective." Either that or maybe her angels *had* worked some magic. "It has to mean that they're feeling better."

David walked along beside her, focusing his full attention on the sound of her hopeful voice and the rumble of the puppies in his pocket. He wasn't going to be the one to tell her that cancer patients often rallied before the end. He wasn't going to point out that Liz and Benjy's conversation had been more in the nature of whispered dreams than boisterous, animated planning. If he couldn't share her fantasies, at least he wasn't going to wrest them from her. And if that compromised his professional position, obligations, and reputation, then it was the lesser of the two evils. As aloof and detached as he tried to seem, he could no more be the one to hurt her now than he could have abandoned the puppies. The knowledge was bittersweet. She'd worked a miracle. In the short time he'd known her, she'd managed to find and breathe life and hope into a heart he'd thought had been amputated right along with his foot. He loved her. And worse, he couldn't seem to stop himself from wishing that she might pull off another miracle and love him in return. It was impossible. But the fact that it was didn't make the wish go away.

"Have you got the puppies situated?" he asked as they put their helmets on.

"They're sleeping on either side of my sweatshirt, right next to my skin." She laughed as one of the puppies moved and tickled her ribs. "I look like I have a spare tire around my middle, especially since I had to tuck the ends into my pants so the puppies wouldn't fall out."

"I'll make this a quick trip." He smiled in spite of himself. "If there's one thing I remember about puppies, it's that they're likely to leave puddles wherever they are."

"Oh, ye gods." He climbed on the motorcycle and waited until she was settled with her arms around his waist and her breasts pushed firmly up against his back before he gunned the engine to life.

She laid her helmeted head against his back, and hugged him tighter as they took off for the camp. "Do I have to choose between going slow and having the puppies wet my pants, or going fast and . . ." She hid her face and closed her eyes as he leaned into a corner, her body striving to make itself one with him wherever they touched.

David opened his visor and let the fifty-five-mile-an-hour wind in his face blow the cobwebs and doubts away for the moment. Maybe he wasn't a knight on a charger. But if her thinking of him that way resulted in this, then he was going to keep his black leather armor ready and his motorized charger in tune.

He would undoubtedly regret it later, but for now it was worth it to feel her against him, to have her with him. Having that was worth going through anything, even the wet puddles spreading from both of his jacket pockets down onto his jeans.

Eight

"Why, Counselor Ortega, it looks like you have an awful case of the mumps." Angela laughed softly as she watched David's "mumps" moving around inside the partially zipped motorcycle jacket.

"Wet mumps," he whispered as they tiptoed through the hospital corridors.

"Wet, noisy mumps." She coughed to cover up the tiny yips emanating from his clothes.

"Tell me again how I got stuck with all four of the little beasts?" He reached one hand around to move one of the particularly active lumps up front. The puppy stuck its wet nose out of the top of the jacket and began chewing on a button, making Angela laugh and David curse.

"You know I couldn't carry them," she said. "Their claws kept getting stuck in the sweatshirt material."

"I have news for you." He gritted his teeth as they rounded the corner on Liz and Benjy's floor, thankful that the home stretch was in sight. "Their claws and teeth are now getting stuck into my skin, along with their wet noses."

"Try to remember how much Liz and Benjy are going to enjoy them." She peered cautiously behind them, then again at the stretch of corridor ahead. She whistled in relief that no one was in sight. She wasn't sure even she could bribe her way out of bringing puppies into a hospital.

"I have been thinking about how much they're going to like the puppies," David admitted quietly, showing her his softer side for just a moment before hiding it away again, like a turtle seeking the safety of its shell. "That's the only reason I haven't tossed these unhousebroken, flea-ridden, drooling mutts into a gunnysack full of rocks myself."

"Oh, yeah?" She gave him a knowing look. He wasn't half as hard as he pretended to be.

"Yeah," he lied gruffly. "Don't imagine for a minute that I'm doing this for you. There's no telling where things would lead if I started doing that. One day you're drawing dragons without permission; the next we're importing illegal puppies into a supposedly near sterile environment. If I don't watch myself, you'll have me gluing horns on our ponies and parading them around as unicorns."

"Unicorns?" she repeated speculatively. "You know, that's not a bad idea. We could—"

"*We could not.*" He fished two of the puppies out of his jacket and put them into her hands. "You're going to have your hands full, as it is, explaining to the head nurse why you're trying to smuggle contraband into her hospital." He veered to one side as an Amazon of a woman in a crisp white uniform marched down the corridor toward them.

"What are doing?" Angela asked as she balanced the wriggling puppies against her chest.

"Preparing to run the fifty-yard dash."

"What for? You work here too. Staff psychologist must have some leverage."

"Not where this head nurse is concerned," he replied in an ominously low voice.

"Now you tell me! Couldn't you just say that the puppies are an important psychological tool in the children's therapy?"

"It would take an act of God to convince this head nurse to bend her rules. Psychological mumbo jumbo doesn't work with her. She's told me to stuff it before."

"And you put up with that?"

"Look at her!" David said and chuckled. "Do I have a choice? I can't run as fast as I used to."

Angela glared at the voice of experience. "So now what do we do?" The nurse was almost upon them and there wasn't an act of God in sight.

"You're going to run interference for me while I take these fellas to Liz and Benjy. At least this way they'll get two out of four." He grinned at her and pulled his two charges out of their hiding place, holding one in each hand like footballs. "I'll tell Benjy that his pup is the new soccer mascot and that he's in charge of taking care of him. And I'll tell Liz that you gave your life to make sure they got behind the enemy lines. What do you think? Sound good?"

It sounded wonderful. Maybe it wouldn't last longer than it took to get the bootleg puppies to their final destination. But he was enjoying this. She could see it from the expression on his face and the light in his eyes. There was hope there and an impish sense of illicit adventure that made him appear more Tom Sawyer than Sigmund Freud. The love she felt for him welled up, strong and fiercely protective. She decided she was going to have to learn the fine art of defensive tackling posthaste, because David and his black-market pets were going to get past the head nurse, even if it meant taking said nurse out by the knees. Angela readied herself for the confrontation. After engaging dragons in battle, how much more difficult could one head nurse be?

Drawing the woman's attention to herself by waving the now barking pups in the air, she waved David by. *Go for it!* She mentally willed him on, smiling triumphantly as he skated into Liz and Benjy's room.

"I'll just bet you think these are real puppies, right?" She held one of the animals under the head nurses's nose. "Isn't it amazing what they can do these days with rubber, plastic, and fake fur? See? They even smell like the real thing. They move. They bark. They . . . wet."

The jig was up. Barring that act of God, she was going to have to make a run for it or she would end up with two puppies inside a gunnysack full of rocks at the bottom of some pond.

"Ms. Newman, I believe we're going to need to speak to the director." The head nurse was not amused.

Angela tensed her running muscles just as the nearest thing to God in camp emerged from the ward just beyond—living proof that miracles did exist. It was the director with Sylvia Krisik at his side. "Hi!" She waved at the large black woman and her administrative companion with undisguised relief. Reinforcements. Possible deliverance. These were two people who'd proven themselves human enough to understand pleading, logic, tears, or if worse came to worse, bribery.

"Director, Sylvia." She nodded to both as she launched into an explanation that would cover all the bases. "There's been a very minor misunderstanding here involving hospital rules. Now, I understand there are perfectly good reasons to have rules. But I think that under special circumstances, we could perhaps bend—" She stopped in the middle of her explanation, a puzzled frown on her face. The director was looking at her with a pity and understanding she hadn't done anything to deserve yet. And what was wrong with Sylvia? There was no smile, no sparkle in her dark eyes today.

"Is something wrong with Liz?" she queried sharply.

"Liz is about the same," the director replied.

"Then what?" Something was terribly wrong. The hair on the back of her neck and arms prickled warningly.

"I'll let Sylvia fill you in on the rest." He motioned for the head nurse to follow him. "I have some phone calls to make and a few details to see to, so please excuse me."

Angela watched as he and the now docile Amazon of a nurse walked briskly back to the nurses' station.

"I'm going to see Liz." Angela ran down the hall, the forgotten puppies still in her hands.

Sylvia reached the door first and put her arm out to stop Angela from entering. "Angela, it's important that you listen to me." The friendly, slow, syrupy tones that Angela had come to associate with Sylvia's voice were absent. When she spoke now, it was with the crisp, clear voice of command authority. "As the director told you, Liz is no worse than she was when you left here this morning. In fact, as you may have been told, she's been put on the same experimental medication as Benjy. That she's able to rest without her earlier symptoms is a good sign. That's why I'd rather you didn't go in now. She's finally sleeping peacefully, and I can't have her getting upset all over again."

"All over again?" Two and two were not adding up to the expected four. Angela hadn't slept all night, but surely her brain wasn't that muzzy. "I don't understand. I'm not going to upset her. David and I just wanted to bring these puppies to her and Benjy. I don't see how a couple of puppies could upset her."

"That's what I'm trying to tell you." Sylvia put a rock-solid hand on her shoulder. "Liz was with Benjy just before he fell asleep and slipped into a coma. We had to life-flight him to a bigger hospital near his family doctor and his parents."

"But he's going to live," Angela said steadily, refusing to allow even a quaver to turn the flat statement into a hint of question.

Slyvia didn't answer the statement directly. "It's unfortunate, but it appears as though the medication simply didn't have the time to work. He was an awfully sick little boy."

"He still is." Angela's voice had risen sharply. Benjy wasn't dead!

Sylvia took the puppies. "Yes."

Angela held her hands up to her ears to still the dragon's near victorious roar. *It wasn't supposed to be this way!* She had to see Liz. She had to find a way to convince the little girl that she wasn't going to end up in the same condition as her friend.

"I should have been here," she mumbled, unaware that Sylvia was watching her intently yet sympathetically. "Liz has needed me three times and I haven't been there for her—when she first came here, then last night on the mountain, and now. I can't let her down again. I've *got* to see her."

Sylvia hesitated and then finally nodded, pushing the door to Liz's room open only enough for Angela to peek inside. "Liz is all talked out for now," she whispered softly, barely moving her lips. "I stayed with her and talked to her until she fell asleep. She'll sleep the rest of the night now, and she needs to if the medication is going to have a chance to work."

Angela looked at her niece through frightened eyes, seeing clearly now a possibility that she had never really allowed herself to consider before. "She could go the same way as Benjy, couldn't she? And there's nothing I can to do stop it!"

Sylvia pulled her back from the room and quietly closed the door. "You have to help yourself before you can help her. It won't do her any good to see you out of control and having hysterics."

"But I *am* out of control." Angela felt free to confide her anguish now. "And I can't help!"

"Oh, yes you can." Sylvia guided her to a nearby waiting room and poured her a cup of coffee. "You've already helped Benjy, and, in a way, Liz too. Do you know what they were doing right before Benjy fell asleep and then slipped into the coma?"

A memory tickled her brain. "Something about planning a costume party?"

"We hold a costume party-dance at camp once a month." Sylvia nodded. "Benjy and Liz were on his bed, planning what to wear. They were going to come as angels, copying their costumes after the angels you'd drawn for Benjy and hung around their room. Right before he went to sleep, he opened his eyes and spoke to Liz. He said: 'I can see my angel. And she really is beautiful, just like your aunt said she'd be.' When the nurse tried to wake him up for his medication a little later, your paper angel was in his arms. We tucked it into his blankets before we put him on the helicopter."

Angela bit her lower lip, willing herself to concentrate on that pain instead of the pain she felt for Benjy. She waited for Sylvia to go on, not trusting herself to speak without crying.

"Don't you see?" Sylvia shook her arm to make the point. "Benjy may die. But you've helped make it possible for him to go without fear, and you've helped Liz, too, in that way. In the end, after we had done all we could with medicine and counseling, you and your magic optimism, your rainbow-under-every-cloud philosophy, and your loving, sunshiny, fairy-tales-can-come-true personality gave him something we could not. You gave him something he could take with him—a guardian angel to light his way. It was real for him." She gave Angela a long, unfathomable look. "Maybe it was real. I don't know. but I do know that he might never have seen her without you to tell him to look. I know that, because of what you did and because of what Benjy said, if and when Liz needs a guardian angel, she'll know to look too." She rubbed the puppies' heads and went over to the vending machine to buy some milk to give to them . . . and to permit Angela to have some time to think about what she'd said.

"It's not the miracle you wanted," Sylvia conceded after the puppies were settled with their milk. "But it's as strong as any magic mortal man can weave," she added pointedly. "In any case, you've done all you can tonight for Liz and for Benjy. They don't need you now. But I think I know of someone who does, someone you might be able to work a real miracle on, if you're interested."

A flash of nonverbal communication between the two women brought the same name to their lips. "David," they both said at once.

"Where is he? He went into the room before I did. He was so eager to give Benjy the puppy that he left me behind." Images of what he must have seen and felt upon going into the room to find Benjy's empty bed filled her mind. She left the untasted coffee sitting on the waiting-room table and rose to her feet. "Where is he now?"

Sylvia shook her head regretfully. "I haven't the foggiest idea. I was just getting Liz to sleep when he burst in. By the time I extricated myself, one of the floor nurses had told him about Benjy. It was only a matter of a minute or so, but when I came out of the room, he was gone. No one seemed to know where." She pressed her lips together in worry. "I know how fond he was of that little fellow. I don't like to think of David being alone now."

"He won't be alone for long," Angela promised. As Sylvia had said, David was someone she *could* do something for, if she could find him. A feeling of grim determination replaced those of impotent anguish within her.

Sylvia picked the puppies up, and said she would look after them for the night as Angela wouldn't have time. She smiled just a little then. "When you find David, tell him Benjy wanted him to come to the party as a pirate in honor of their soccer team, the Pirates. He wanted to pin this on David's chest." She transferred both puppies to one hand and pulled a construction-paper "medal" out of her pocket with the other. Roughly cut and colored to resemble a pirate, the block-printed words underneath read: Number 1 Pirate, coach and friend. Love, Benjy.

Angela took the treasure and put it carefully into her pocket. A long, long time ago when life had started burying her in lemons, she had decided that she was going to make lemonade with a vengeance. Now she had to see to it that David learned how to like lemonade too.

Of course, she had to find him first. And that might prove to be the most difficult task of all. Sylvia had been right. He had disappeared. In a puff of smoke, along with two puppies.

Angela pulled a camp map out of her pocket and checked off all the places she had looked for David—his cabin, the Fun Center, the cafeteria, his office, the hospital again, several of the boys' cabins. David would need more than food and water if he still had the pups: he'd need to be fumigated. "Think, Angela, think!" She yawned, almost eating the pencil she'd been resting her chin on. Where was he? She'd been to all the main drags in camp, but there were innumerable off-the-beaten-track places that he might be holed up in. But which one? She rubbed tired eyes, dismissing the possibility that if he was hiding in some out-of-the-way place, it probably indicated that he very much wanted to be alone.

"One more place," she promised her bone-weary muscles and aching feet. "Just one more place and I'll quit until morning. Which does not"—she shook her fist in the air and lectured the oak trees aloud—"which, I repeat, does not give you the license to rape and pillage during the night, you damnable dragons!"

She nodded her obviously addlepated head. She was beginning to get punch-drunk with fatigue. She was beginning to see dragons around every corner, and hear puppies in the . . . trees? There is was again. She tilted her head back to look up. There, maybe fifteen feet up in the tangle of oak tree limbs was a tree house. Moreover, there were definitely puppy sounds coming from within. Could David be up there as well? There was only one way to find out.

Carefully picking her way up the rickety planks that had been inexpertly nailed to the trunk, she finally reached the platform and flung herself over the top. The puppies rushed over to her and, falling all over themselves in glee, began the intimate process of washing her face.

"Yech!" she said and hastily made it to all fours and scooted over to where a silent David sat, hunched over, with his back to her.

"David?" she queried gently. Was he asleep? Was he comatose? Was he alive? "David, are you all right?" She put one hand on his trembling back, wanting and yet not knowing how to help him. "David, my sweet, talk to me." She put both hands on his back now, caressing soothing circles from his collarbone down around his shoulder blades and back up again. The trembling increased, and still he didn't speak. "David, love, let me *in*. I want to help. Don't shut me out." She put her head against the middle of his back and let her arms slide around to his stomach.

He was visibly shaking now, his mind and his heart stricken with a seizure of pain so intense that it carried over to his body.

She held him. She held on, and she held fast to the things she believed in even as she felt the salty wetness of his tears fall onto her arms.

"I'm here," she promised in a reassuring whisper. "I'm here for you. I need you too."

"No you don't." The anger inside of him exploded. He flung himself away from her embrace. "You're not here for *me*. You came to find some imagined knight in shining armor." He wrapped his arms around his shivering body. "And you don't need me. What you want is for me to wave a magic sword over everything and tell you it's all going to be all right. Well, I can't do that." He looked up at her then, his eyes red-rimmed and haunted, empty of everything but torment. "I can't be anybody's knight in shining armor, and I'm sure as hell not God! I can't slay dragons, I can't perform miracles, and I can't make anyone's dreams come true, not even my own!"

Angela leaned against the tree trunk for support, not afraid of him, but of the desolation she could see inside of him. She hesitated for just a moment. She could play it safe and go. She could leave the tree house and him and what was growing between them behind. She could abandon her white knight to the dragons. Or she could stay and fight for him. She could fight with him against their common enemy.

There was really no choice. She was in love with him. And she could no more abandon him than she could abandon her ideals. "*That's* the trouble with you, Almost Doctor Know-It-All." She let her own anger at fate out on him, using its passion to give her the energy to hold his attention. "You are a lily-livered quitter, that's what you are. You give up too soon. And because of that, I'm inclined to believe that maybe you're right. Maybe you can't make your own dreams come true. But I happen to know that you're the only person who can make somebody else's come true. And I'm not talking about me right now," she added as he opened his mouth to deny what she was saying. "I'm talking about Benjy." She pulled the paper medallion out and pinned it to his shirt. "He made this for you today because he hoped he'd be here to pin it on you tomorrow at the costume party. He made it for you because, to him, you were the same kind of hero that you are to me—a knight, a pirate, larger than life." She wiped at a tear. She was not going to cry! She wasn't finished yet, and there was no time for it. "It doesn't matter whether you believe it or not. He believed it. He still does. Dammit, David, he's in a coma, but he's not dead, and I'm not going to stand for you mourning for him as if you've given up. And I'm not going to let the dragons hold a victory celebration prematurely. And, so help me, if I have to dress you up in a scarlet sash and a black eye patch myself, and drag you kicking and swearing all the way, you're going to appear at that costume party just as Benjy wanted you to. And furthermore, you're going to swash and buckle your way around while I take pictures for Benjy to see later or I'll . . . I'll make you walk the plank!"

David towered over the top of her, bristling like a hedgehog with its quills rubbed the wrong way. His eyes had narrowed to slits, and he was still shaking, but now it was with anger.

"The hell you say, woman!" he bellowed. "You and what army? Who appointed you to be the keeper of my conscience? For that matter, who appointed you my social secretary and invited you to invade my privacy?"

"Maybe I'm *your* guardian angel," she snapped. "Maybe I'm here to make sure you don't forget how to dream. But in any case, whatever else I am and whatever else I do, tomorrow night I'm going to be the one who sees to it that Bluebeard dances a jig at that costume party."

"Yeah?" He dug his mental heels in, not sure why he was doing so except that it felt awfully good to have some control over something. "What if I told you that I haven't danced a jig or anything else in over a year, and that I've never even been to one of the camp costume parties?"

"Then I'd say it was high time you went to one." She stood unafraid of his challenge, with her feet apart and her hands on her hips, her flashing eyes fixed directly on him. "Oh, I know you've lost your foot, and that's probably why you haven't gone to the dance. But you're going to this one, unless, along with your foot, they amputated your heart and your guts and—"

Angela found herself crushed in a fierce embrace that didn't slack up as David lowered them both to the floor of the tree house.

"I've got a heart." He ground the admission out in between hard, almost bruising kisses. "And I've got guts. . . ." His kiss gentled then as other emotions took over, replacing his anger. "And I *must* have a guardian angel, because I've still got you even though, with everything I've done and said to you, I shouldn't have." He smoothed her hair back so that he could see her face. "Do you want to tell me why you left Liz to come looking for me? It must have been pretty important."

"It is important," she agreed readily. "I came because I love you." She looked deeply into his eyes, willing him to believe. "I love *you*, David

Ortega. And I do need you. I need you to love me. I need you to make love to me."

He groaned and pulled her into as intimate contact as he could with their clothes and the puppies in the way. For the moment he was filled with needs and desires that were stronger than his reservations. For the time being she, they were all that mattered. She loved him. She loved him! If this was a dream, he never wanted to wake up!

"Yessssss." He fought to keep himself from ripping her clothes off and taking her right there amid the leaves, acorns, and puppies. "We'll make love. But not here." He hoisted her to her feet before either one of them could change their minds. "I'm sure a good psychologist could come up with a perfectly legitimate reason to make love in a tree house. But I doubt a pirate could and I'm absolutely certain that a knight in shining armor couldn't."

He helped her down to the ground and jumped down beside her with a flourish, his expression open, revealing his passion and the love for Angela that he could no longer hide. "And tonight, maybe just for tonight, I want to be your knight. I want to find those dreams and make them come true with you."

Nine

Once they'd reached their mutual decision, Angela had assumed everything would be simple from there on out. If it had been left up to her, she'd have flung the doors to his cabin wide and then been in his arms in the next moment. The dogs could wait. Locking the door could wait. The world could wait. But she couldn't wait—not a second longer. It felt as though she'd been waiting a lifetime as it was.

"David, I realize that the history books sometimes portray knights in shining armor as being chaste. But I think there must have been a misprint somewhere along the line. You don't need to take it so literally." She followed him as he set out milk and some leftover taco meat from the refrigerator for the puppies. "I'm sure the word that was meant was *chased*—which, in case you haven't noticed, is what you're being."

He slopped the milk onto the floor, cursed, and smeared it around with his orange tennis shoes. "I just don't want to be eaten by hungry puppies."

"We could lock the bedroom door," she suggested helpfully.

"I don't want my door to be eaten by hungry puppies," he retorted. "Don't forget. It was *your* idea to bring the little beasts home." He paced the confines of his small kitchen once and then snapped his fingers. "Say, are you thirsty? I could make us both a drink."

Angela watched as he ran to the cupboard and began search to its contents before she could tell him that she wasn't thirsty.

"Damn." He slammed the cupboard doors shut and swore again. "I forgot. You drank all my medicinal Scotch the last time you were here."

He was stalling. *He was nervous.* It came to her in a flash. She glanced down at his legs, suddenly remembering that all of their previous intimacy had been inside a sleeping bag in a darkened tent. She had never really seen the man under the orange tennis shoes, so to speak, and he was afraid she might not like what she saw.

"David, I don't have to be half tipsy to want you."

"You never know." He gnawed on a thumbnail for a second and then hurried to another cupboard. "But no matter, I've got just the thing. Cooking sherry." He pulled a half-empty bottle out from next to the seasoned salt and the oregano, dusting it off on his pants. "We can mix this with lemon-lime soda. It'll be great."

Great? It could be lethal. It could be moldy. "Cooking sherry coolers." She resolutely held back a grimace. "Sounds wonderful."

He looked relieved. "We can have them in the bedroom . . . by candlelight." Digging around in a bottom drawer, he pulled out an open package of birthday candles.

"We can if we can find our glasses in the dark." She squinted at the candles. "I never knew they made holders that small." She took the six candles in her hand and reached for the cooking sherry as he rummaged in the refrigerator for soda and ice.

"No matter." He backed out of the refrigerator, mixers in hand. "If we can't make them stand up, we can always drink in the dark."

She followed him into the bedroom, wishing she knew of some way to make him feel comfortable before he communicated his nervousness to her.

"Which is probably a better idea," he continued with his monologue. "That way you won't see the spots on the jelly jars I use for wineglasses." He took several quick, deep breaths. Composure was impossible. The best he could hope for was controlled hysteria. And it did no good to tell himself that she wasn't the first woman he'd made love to since he'd lost his foot. She was the first woman he'd *loved* since then. And moreover, she was the first woman he'd needed to love him in return. Why did he have to fall in love with a woman who continued to see him as some perfect story-book knight that he could never be? What was she going to do once she saw that the reality didn't live up to the illusion? How was he going to get out of this before that happened?

"I forgot the jelly jars." He made a break for the door. "I'll get them." He went back into the kitchen to ponder the dilemma, leaving her momentarily alone in the darkened bedroom.

Angela slipped out of her shoes and sat gingerly

on his bed, wishing, for just a moment, that he had made love to her up in the tree house. It was one thing to be swept off one's feet. It was one thing to be overcome with impulsive passion. It was quite another to have to do the seducing oneself, especially when one had such limited experience. Didn't they have their roles reversed? They probably did. But she didn't think reminding him of it was going to help.

"I'm going to have to wash one of these glasses," he called out to her from the kitchen. "Unless you want to try cooking sherry and grape jelly coolers."

"No, thanks," she called back to him as glassware clattered in the sink. "Just take your time. I'm going to look for something to put the candles in."

With a flash of inspiration she dashed into his bathroom and found a cake of soap by the sink. That ought to work to hold the candles upright. She was about to leave when another idea occurred to her. It always worked in the movies. She contemplated his shower. Why not?

Sticking the candles in their makeshift holder, she lit them and undressed, throwing her clothes off in button-popping haste.

"What *are* you doing?" she heard him ask amid the clatter and crash of falling glass as she turned his shower on high.

"Washing the puppy fur and fleas off my delicate self," she shouted before stepping into the shower and pulling the glass door partially closed.

"You didn't need to do that." His voice sounded closer, as if his own curiosity and desire had forced him to investigate in spite of his nerves.

"I did unless you want to spray me with Raid," she said as he stepped into the birthday-candle-lit bathroom. "I hope you don't mind if I use your shampoo too."

Mind? "I don't mind." He could see the outlines of her body through the steam-frosted glass, thinking how much she resembled a lithe water sprite in soapy suds. What right did he have to take a water sprite?

"You could join me if you wanted to." Somehow it always sounded better in the movies, coming from some tall, leggy blond who was sexy for a living. "I could always wash your back." And his front . . . and if he said no she was going to quietly slither down the drain.

"David?" She wiped a small spot on the shower door after a few moments had passed, and tried to see if he was still there. "Are you still out there?"

"I'm out here." And he still hadn't made a decision about what to do, about what to tell her. "I'm still out here."

"I know *that*." She leaned her head against the glass of the door. "What I don't know is why you're not in here." She listened to the dead silence. Oh, this was wonderful, she thought to herself. This was the last time she was going to try to seduce anybody.

"I guess because I know I won't be able to think straight if I come in." He moved closer to the door. "I won't be able to have second thoughts. I'm so tempted to come in now that I'm forgetting all the reasons why I shouldn't."

She dropped a wet washcloth over her face and groaned. "You make showering with me sound like as much fun as being the first soldier to hit the beach on D day."

"I don't mean to do that." His hand curled

around the door. "You have to believe that I *want* to come in."

She covered his hand with hers and gently pulled him closer, still not daring to look at him. "Then do it."

"We may both live to regret this." He pulled his shirt over his head and dropped it to the floor. "But it's too late. I want you too much to do anything else."

She listened to him as he took off the rest of his clothes, but she didn't turn around to face him until he got in beside her. And she wasn't sure if she even breathed until he pulled her against his naked chest.

She shivered in response, her skin prickling with a thousand goose pimples even though the water was steaming hot. It was too dark to see him, but she could feel the coarse hair of his chest, and the hard tips of his small, taut nipples when she pressed her breasts against him. And she could feel the hard thickness of his arousal as he let himself lean against her.

The feeling was sensuous and warm and intimate and—And it felt like a tennis shoe. She lifted one foot to explore his.

"David, do you want to tell me why you're wearing your tennis shoes and therefore your prosthesis in the shower?" She could feel him breathing but he wasn't answering. "David, if you turn catatonic on me again, I'm going to scream."

"I'm wearing it because it's a little hard to carry you to bed on one foot. I'd have to hop," he explained practically. "And because I guess I'm not ready for you to see me yet without my shining armor."

She'd known that was it, of course. What else

could it have been "Is *that* why we've been dancing around like a couple of virgins on our wedding night?" she asked. "Not to worry. This is the age of women's liberation. I'll carry myself to bed, thank you. If you'd like, I'll carry you. . . ." She looked speculatively up and down his six-foot body. "Maybe I'll go cavewoman on you and just drag you there. On second thought, dragging you would take too much time. If it'll make you feel better, I'll blow the candles out, you can get naked, and we can hop into bed together." She leaned out of the shower and blew the birthday candles out.

"Wanton thing." He stepped out of the shower with a silly half grin at her teasing, and lifted her carefully into his arms.

"The bed's over there somewhere, I *think*. The room's so dimly lighted."

"Don't worry." He tried a little experimental joke on himself. "One of the few advantages of my prosthesis is that I've only got half as many toes to stub."

He held her to his chest tightly for a long moment before laying her down on his bed. "I love you," he said simply, baring that piece of his heart to her at last. "And I'm so damned scared that you won't, and that you shouldn't love me in return, that I've spent half our time together here tonight trying to avoid what I've been driving myself crazy for days wanting. Think I ought to find a good counselor?"

"I know a fine one." Angela reached up to pull him down next to her on the bed. "He's intelligent"—she traced a finger around his high, intelligent forehead—"and sensitive." The stroking finger slipped down over the bridge of his nose, past his lips and chin, and went straight to his heart. "And I'm not sure that it counts, but he's quite a hunk too!" She grabbed him in a bear hug and rolled over and over on the bed with him trapped within her embrace. "And he's the first, last, and only man I've ever known who's exactly what every woman dreams her hero will be like."

"All that *and* a fair-to-middling psychologist too?" He rescued a pillow that was ready to fall off the bed and put it under her head so that their faces were only inches apart.

She lifted her lips fractionally until they came into contact with his, pouring her love for him out in half-sentence kisses. "Yup. And he's the only man"—she paused to kiss him again—"only man I could ever imagine living happily ever after with."

David closed his eyes for a second, savoring the sound and the implications of her promise before dashing it to pieces in his mind. He could have the fantasy of tonight. But he couldn't hope for more. He couldn't let himself begin to hope for miracles like that.

When he cupped her face between his hands, they were trembling so much that she could have felt it in his fingers even if she hadn't been able to see his eyes. "Don't promise me forever, Angel. Don't do that to me. Just give me tonight. Let me love you tonight and don't think about tomorrow. But whatever you do, don't promise me a happily-ever-after you can't deliver."

"David, I love you." For her that said it all. She loved him; and wonder of wonders, miracle of miracles, it seemed that the logic-loving, usually down-to-earth, pragmatic man loved her too. Forevers and happily-ever-afters were a foregone conclusion, a given he could accept. Once she had given her love, there was no taking it back, not ever. And if he didn't believe that now, if somewhere in his heart a part of him still expected her to desert him as his fiancée had done, then she was just going to have to find new and inventive ways to prove him wrong.

"Okay for now." She wasn't going to argue with him tonight. "So love me tonight. Love me now."

He was lost, caught up in his own undeniable need for her. "My sweet love, my sweet angel. Yes. Yes, I'll love you tonight." Tonight and forever, as long as they both should live, he added to himself. It was too late to think otherwise. Now, no matter what she did, no matter what promises she did or did not keep, he would still love her. He took her into his arms possessively, determined that if he could only have her for now, perhaps only for this one night, then it was going to be a night of loving like neither of them had ever had before.

What had started out as a spark of desire days ago grew almost instantaneously into a raging firestorm now. Their mouths met and opened to each other on contact, their tongues touching and caressing and tasting each other's special taste in wild abandon.

He splayed the fingers of both his hands and moved them in a slow-motion braille from her graceful neck down to her delicate shoulders. "You must be an angel." He breathed the compliment. "Only an angel's skin could be this soft. Only an angel's hair could smell this good." He buried his face in her wet curls and breathed deeply, moving around to nuzzle her neck and suck on the sensitive lobe of her ear.

"Sweet nothings . . . sweet nothings . . . sweet nothings . . ."

She could practically hear him smile. "I've never had anybody whisper sweet nothings in my ear before. It's nice." Leaning over, she caressed his back and shoulders with yearning hands, and licked a sweet nothing of her own in Morse code around his ears and down his neck. "Did you get my message, love?"

He made a low growling sound deep in his throat and, wrapping his arms around her waist, rolled her back toward the middle of the bed. She ended up sitting on top of him. "Are you getting mine?"

Angela shuddered involuntarily as his hard male body rubbed against her innermost thighs and at the moist entrance to her femininity. She lowered her head to his chest, dragging the curtain of her hair over his face, and moaned.

Her hair tickled erotically and sent shivers of longing up and down his spine. Her throaty acknowledgment of their mutual desire thrilled him even more. "Angel, sit up and let me look at you." He exhaled raggedly. "Let me see you. Please. I've never seen a naked angel before, and I want to see what one looks like in the flesh." An image he could hold in his thoughts and in his dreams forever, long after the real one had gone.

Angela felt her heartbeat increase, racing to keep up with her quickened breathing. There was a time to be Pollyanna and a time to be Pandora, and just this once she was determined to get it right. Brushing a heavy wave of her hair back off one shoulder, she bared one full breast proudly in the moonlit room, and left the other to peek provocatively out from under the tumble of curls. Rocking with a gentle rhythm back and forth, she let her hand slide down and follow the hourglass curves of her breast and waist and hip, bringing it to rest at last on his flat stomach. Never breaking eye contact, she did the same with her other hand until it too rested at his waist. Pushing herself down the length of his body with an excruciating lack of haste, she finally stopped at a point that left her lips even with the triangular patch of hair at his groin. She smiled up at him with a contented-cat kind of satisfaction, her lips enticingly near the throbbing proof of his own love and desire.

"Touch me, Angel." He swallowed convulsively, his fists gripping the covers at his side.

She traced a soft, stroking pattern on his swollen flesh with her fingers. "It's Pandora, David. I'm not an angel tonight. But you are most definitely my knight of steel." She kissed him intimately, taking as much pleasure in the giving as he did in the receiving. When she raised her head at his guttural cry, her eyes were luminous with love for him.

"But now I want to see the rest of you. I want to see the man under the armor." She caressed his upper thighs and slowly lowered her hands to his knees and then lower still. "I love you, David. I love your body." She raised her eyebrows at his suggestive expression. "And not just the obvious parts. I love all the bumps and freckles and scars and moles. There isn't a single part of you that I wouldn't love just the same as all the others."

She touched his artificial leg, still clad in a sock and its orange tennis shoe. "Let me take this off now. I promise I won't make you chase me around the bedroom. In fact, I think I'd really prefer it if you couldn't get away very quickly. I think you're a very special man, and I don't think I could stand it if you ran out on me." She stripped one shoe and sock off and dropped them to the floor, drying his so recently showered foot on a towel they'd dropped beside the bed. The artificial foot was next, and she lowered the sock covering it with great care, going slowly enough to give David time to get used to the idea. He clenched and unclenched his hands several times as if preventing what she was doing was an impulse hard to control. But at last he held still, his body rigid and waiting.

The prosthesis came off with a minimum of effort. She set it gently aside, and dried and massaged the part of his leg that remained. Perfectly proportioned in all other ways, his one leg simply ended six inches or so below his knee. Impulsively, she leaned over and kissed him there with the same love and admiration that she had devoted to the rest of his body.

"I know you want me to say that I love you in spite of this physical difference." She held his leg in loving hands, petting and stroking him easily. "But to me, that's a little like having to say that I'll love you when you have wrinkles or gray hair or you become hard of hearing or nearsighted or, heaven forbid, *old*. I'll say it if you want me to, but I'm telling you now that it's something you can take for granted." She shrugged. "I'm not trying to downplay its importance, but I honestly don't see anything about you that makes it hard to love you . . . with or without your armor."

The stiff expression on his face crumpled for a brief second, composed itself and broke again, running the emotional gamut from bittersweet sadness to relief to gratitude to joy and finally to something that had no name, but which she understood without a need for words.

"I never thought I'd believe in miracles again." His voice was tight with unshed tears. "But lady of my heart, you are a genuine miracle, and you've more than made my dreams come true. You *are* my dreams come true."

Angela let her head fall back in exaltation as he sat up and pressed her body against his. Never, never in her wildest dreams had she loved or been loved this way. In comparison to David the men in her past and the heroes in her imagination were colorless, flat, and one-dimensional. He drove them one and all from her mind in the next few minutes, replacing insipid fantasy with vivid reality, supplanting bland, lackluster experience with something so powerful it shook her to the very depths of her being.

He loved her with everything he had. He loved her with everything he was. And the knowledge that he did made it possible for her to give him the same in return. Clenching her fists in his hair, she moaned in ecstacy as he found and suckled her breasts, bringing both nipples into his mouth simultaneously. The sensations shot down from her breasts to her pelvis, gathering and building until she ached for more than vicarious stimulation. Thrusting her hips forward, she teased him with her body, engaging him in a flirtatious dance that ended as he dropped lower and parted her legs to kiss her there. Sensations sweeter and more intense than any she had ever known washed over her like a tidal wave, taking her higher and higher until she was dizzy with the height of her passion. She cried out his name and pushed his mouth away from her body. She was building to a finale that would be like no other, and she wanted him with her.

"David, take me now, love me *now*." Digging her fingers into the taut muscles of his arms and back, she drew him forward until at last he reached the hot haven of her desire and thrust himself home.

"Angel, I love you!"

"David, I love you too!"

Riding the waves of their passion as one, it wasn't long before they created their own private miracle and forged their dreams together.

Ten

It had been a night of magic and miracles, a night of desires and dreams come true. It had been like seeing a sky full of rainbows after a terrible storm, a harbinger of things to come.

It had been too perfect to keep to herself. With her creative urges stimulated and running on high, she had left David's bed in the wee hours of the morning, placing a love note on her pillow. And, getting the keys to the cafeteria from the night janitor, she had found her art supplies and had set to work. Taking Liz and Benjy's original ideas for the dance and adding to them, she'd worked alone until potential volunteers had begun filtering into the cafeteria cum dance hall for breakfast.

By the time everyone had broken for lunch, the room had been transformed into a three-dimensional fantasy from one of her stories. Sylvia and her art class, who had been going to do some of the minor decorating, had been kept busy making Puff-the-Magic-Dragon-type dragons to fly from the ceiling, along with griffins and a winged horse.

Cafeteria workers, campers, groundskeepers, and maids had been drafted to make and hang construction-paper hearts and rainbows from wall-to-wall crepe-paper streamers. She'd even managed to convince a few of the administrators to help, using a combination of friendly cajoling, sincere pleading, and executive manipulation to add to her work force.

By the time a baffled David had arrived, a cardboard-and-plywood castle had been erected in one corner of the room and was in the process of being painted along with three walls of cardboard shields and swords.

She'd saved the last wall, the biggest one, for herself. Having awakened the director himself at four A.M. to get permission to paint it in water colors, she'd set to work. And except for checking on Liz and on Benjy's condition periodically, she hadn't stopped since early this morning.

She stood back from it now, a dripping paintbrush hanging from her tired fingers. Viewing the whole for the first time, she smiled in artistic satisfaction. She'd never painted a wall-size mural before, most of her work being scaled down to fit on the pages of a children's storybook. But her style lent itself well to the larger-than-life style and she was more than pleased with the results.

Two main figures dominated the wall: a knight and a dragon, each drawn bigger than anything else in the room. With his pointed tail at one end of the wall and his razor-sharp scales and floor-to-ceiling wings in the middle, and his fearsome head at the other end, the dragon would have been scary if it hadn't been obvious that he was dead. Tiny elflike beings were roasting hot dogs and marshmallows over a smoldering nose that had once breathed fire. Gnomes and fairies stood in line for a turn on the swing that had been strung between his deadly fangs. A white flag of surrender flew from his upturned tail. A flock of angels, some with vaguely familiar features, could be seen floating from the overhead clouds, sprinkling flower petals and glittering pixie dust. And in the center of it all was the knight. She'd drawn him last and with the greatest of care. His armor gleamed like brilliant sunshine, its aura surrounding him from top to bottom. Fiery glints of that same power shot off in all four directions from his cross-shaped sword, which was stuck in the dragon's underbelly. In deference to David's probable preference for privacy, she'd left the visor of the red-plumed helmet down. But the piercing eyes that watched her from the painting were David's. The hands were too. She'd drawn them from memory, strong and tanned and spare of flesh. They bore the scars of other battles. She'd made them look fully capable of everything from sheltering butterflies to tearing dragons limb from limb. They were doing neither of these things in the mural. No longer needing to wield the crumpled shield at his side, or the deadly sword, one hand was holding a white satin lady's favor while the other was reaching out to that unseen lady in the painting. The battle was won. The dragon had lost.

Angela dropped the paintbrush into a nearby can of water, and dared a glance at the real knight, whom she'd drafted several hours earlier. He'd finished rearranging and building props for the party, and was now helping decorate some early-bird costumed children.

"Well, Michelangelo?" an impatient David demanded as she glanced at his peevish expression.

"If you're finished with the Sistine Chapel over there, would you mind giving us untalented finger painters over here a hand?"

How long had he been standing there watching her paint? She looked in sympathetic amusement at several of his victims. He'd been watching her a long, long time if his artwork was any indication. Nobody could paint that badly and have his eyes on what he was painting.

"Couldn't you please help?" David's living canvas pouted with green-tinged lips. "I'm supposed to be a leprechaun, and he's made me look like a warty toad."

"A deformed warty toad," David agreed grimly.

Angela laughed at the warty toad and its creator before whisking the instrument of torture from David's fingers. "Maybe he's just never seen a leprechaun before." She laughed again as she dipped the paintbrush in green paint and began repairing the damage. "You have to believe in them to see them, you know, and Counselor Ortega *didn't even believe in angels until last night.* So you have to forgive him."

"I will if you can fix me," the warty toad agreed conditionally.

"Don't worry." She wiped little globs of green paint off his face with a tissue. Not enough in some places and too much in others. "I'll make you look so much like a leprechaun that people are going to be after you all evening hoping you'll lead them to your hidden pot of gold." Finishing with him, she looked askance at David as he motioned another candidate for a bath from the cafeteria door.

"Wait just a minute," she protested. "I don't have time to do everybody in camp. I have to go over and see Liz. I've called the hospital several times in the last couple of hours, but she's either been asleep or the doctors have been with her every time I've called." She frowned, having been so involved in the painting that she hadn't altogether processed that information until now. "I must have caught her before she woke up and then again when she took a mid-morning nap. Sylvia did say she had to sleep, but that seems like an awful lot of sleep, don't you think?"

"Hard to tell." David looked down at the newest human easel, concentrating on the child's head, left bald from chemotherapy. He knew the symptoms of each kind of cancer and its treatment better than most people at the camp. He'd studied it with a voracious interest only a year ago. When parents asked the kind of questions Angela was asking about their kids, most of the time he knew as many of the answers as their doctors did, and he knew how to make the telling easier. He didn't have any easy answers now, not for either of them.

"David?" She looked at him curiously, letting green paint drip from her fingers, unnoticed.

"Tell you what," he said, "I have to be at the hospital myself in just a little while. Why don't I check on Liz's condition for you and then give you a call. Are you going to be here most of the afternoon?"

"No." She looked at the pleading faces gathered by the door. "Well, maybe just for a while." She hesitated. "David, I want to see Liz in person. I want to see for myself that she's going to be all right." She shrugged. "Of course, I *know* that she's going to be all right, but I want to see if she's going to feel up to coming to the costume party tonight. You see, I have this idea for an angel's costume, but I need to fit it to her."

He cocked a disbelieving eyebrow. "Surely anybody who can paint an entire mural in one morning is talented enough to make an angel's suit without exact measurements."

Why was he trying to keep her away from the hospital? The question flashed through her mind and then fled as he began walking out the door. "David, I'm not going to have time to guess her measurements. It's got to be right the first time because you've screwed up so many kids that it's going to take me all day just to do repairs. I won't have time to do alterations." She was talking to an empty doorway. David had gone, leaving a line of woebegone variations of the warty toad in his wake.

She sighed in resignation and studied the poorly painted clown who'd come to stand beside her. Even the greasepaint couldn't hide his sad expression. "You won't have to repair more than a dozen of us," the sad-faced clown informed her. "The rest decided to do their own makeup after they got a good look at us."

Angela chuckled in spite of her worry and set to work, applying greasepaint and powder in such a way that the colors didn't run together like a wax candle left out in the sun too long. "There." She held a mirror up for the clown to see himself. "Is that better?"

He assured her that it was and skipped happily to the door, slapping the hand of the next one there like a relay racer.

"Do you think there's *anything* you can do to make me look good for the party?" A little girl looked up at her hopefully. "I've got this no-hair head with a big scar right on top." She shyly withdrew a scarf from her head to reveal the problem. "I don't think you're going to be able to hide it with paint, but I'm sick of the scarf, so can you think of something?"

"And what about me?" Another, older girl spoke up from the door. "I don't even want to go to the dance if I have to go looking like this. They'd think I was the wolfman or something." She lifted up a baseball cap to reveal a few tufts of scraggly hair.

Angela looked longingly in the direction of the hospital before putting the idea of a visit anytime in the next couple of hours out of her mind. She sighed. Well, there was more than one way to skin a dragon.

She contemplated each child in turn with an artist's keen eye. Another of David's clowns was declared a loss, scrubbed, and drawn again. Using her paints in a different way, she dyed the tufts of hair which remained on the teenage "wolfman's" head, coloring them in vivid oranges and purples before spraying them into spikes. With suggestions about tinfoil, paperclip, and safety-pin jewelry, she sent the newly decorated punk rocker on her way, promising to look for a leather jacket to complete the outfit before the party. She painted a big red heart on the other child's completely bald head, then outlined and used the scar to signify where a Cupid's arrow had pierced it. Waving good-bye to a pleased Saint Valentine, she washed her hands in preparation for the next hopeful, and spent the following two hours creating angels and fairies, punk rockers and clowns, and creatures that nobody had ever dreamed of before today. When the last of them was done, she almost flew to the hospital, her hands still streaked with splotches of greasepaint.

She hadn't seen Liz today, and nothing, not even a much-needed bath, was going to keep her from seeing her niece now. Hastily rehearsing an excuse, she hurried down the hall and into Liz's room, expecting to see an angry angel wanting to know what had happened to her wings.

"Now, Liz, I don't want you to get all upset. I haven't *quite* got your angel's outfit down yet, but all I need is a tiny piece of material to finish it, and I can run into town as soon as I borrow someone's car, and get what I need at a yardage shop. By the time the party starts this evening—" The rest of the explanation died on her lips as she walked around to see Liz's face. Lying on her side in the bed, she had appeared to Angela at first to be pouting. But she wasn't pouting. She wasn't even awake. Curled up and small and oh-so-still, she was frighteningly pale. With the exception of the dark circles under her eyes, her face was the color of white bread dough. Her breathing was so quiet, Angela had to get close even to detect it. And when she put her hand on the child's face to see if there was a fever, she was struck by the fact that Liz hadn't so much as moved in response to either the words spoken to her or her aunt's touch. How long had this been going on? And why hadn't she been kept informed?

It was the first question she asked of the nurse who hastened in when she pushed the emergency button at Liz's bedside.

"Why don't we talk outside?" The nurse tried to pull her out of the room. "We don't want to wake our patient, now, do we?"

"Wake her?" Angela felt the hysteria rising in her throat. "I don't think a 747 landing right on top of the building could wake her." She propelled them both out of Liz's room. "I want to see Liz's doctor, and I want to see him now, and I want to know what he's doing for her. And furthermore, I demand to know why I wasn't kept informed of her obviously deteriorating condition!"

The nurse calmly checked a chart she'd carried into the room, verifying its information and entering more. "Your niece, Ms. Newman, looks the way she does, and is as unresponsive as she is, because as yet the new medication doesn't seem to be working, or at least it is not working as quickly as we would like it to. But her vital signs are stable, and for now there is no reason to push the panic button."

Angela bristled at the mild rebuke. "The hell there isn't." The woman's explanation was professional and concise and so totally devoid of emotion that the woman might just as well have been discussing a computer with a software glitch. The fact that the nurse's forced objectivity made it possible for her to come to work in a place such as this and do her job every day without falling apart was of little comfort. Angela shivered uncontrollably and restrained her anger as much as possible. "Perhaps you don't see Liz's behavior, or lack thereof, to be anything to be concerned about. However, I disagree and I would very much like to discuss my concerns with her doctor. Where might I find him?"

"You won't be able to find him now." The nurse checked her charts and then the wall clock. "He's gone for the afternoon. We have another doctor on hand, of course, but he's less familiar with your niece's case than Dr. Flemming. I do assure you, though, that both doctors are aware of your niece's condition. And I can promise you that we have followed their instructions in regard to her care to the letter. Now, I have rounds to make. But if you still aren't satisfied with your niece's care, I can direct you to one of the staff psychologists. Perhaps they can put your mind at ease."

As if worrying about Liz's life was something that was defined as crazy. One. Two. Three. Four. Five. Six . . . She'd have counted to ten before letting loose with her anger, but there wasn't time for either. Not now. "Fine," she snapped impatiently. "Just point me in the direction of either of the staff psychologists."

"Back down the hall, to your right. It's number eighteen. I believe I saw Sylvia Krisik go in there just a few minutes ago."

Angela turned on her heel and left without saying another word. Finding the room took only a few minutes. Pushing the door open and entering unannounced took seconds. Assimilating what she saw once inside the room seemed to take much, much longer.

Sylvia's round face seemed to register a stunned, surprised expression for the longest time before she moved in slow motion to block Angela's path. She wasn't nearly quick enough to block the view of David beyond.

Sitting on an examining table next to a discarded paper gown, he held himself grimly, stiffly erect as one doctor drew blood from his arm to add to an already extensive collection of tubes on a tray, and another doctor checked his prosthesis for comfort and mobility.

Though fully dressed, he looked vulnerable and naked, and above all, alone, though he and Sylvia had obviously been in the middle of a conversation when she'd first entered the room.

"We'll have the test results for you by this evening, David," one of the doctors said on his way to the door.

"Good lord." Sylvia breathed at last, galvanized into motion as the next doctor swept by with David's blood samples in his hand. "Angela, you shouldn't be here. Why don't you let me take you into the lounge for a cup of coffee until David gets finished here." She put a hand on Angela's shoulder and tried to guide her out of the room. "We can all talk then."

"No. Let her stay." David's voice was ominously harsh. "I know why she's here, and so do you. You might as well let her stay."

"But we can talk about it outside, once you're finished in here," Sylvia argued forcefully, an unspoken communication passing between them in milliseconds.

"It's not going to work, Sylvia." He rolled his sleeves and pant legs down and refastened the orange tennis shoes. Lifting himself gingerly off the table, he walked over to where Angela was still staring, openmouthed, at the entire proceeding. "She can't encase her illusions in concrete forever to protect them from harm. Sooner or later we all have to deal with things as they are instead of how we wish they were." The argument fell, prerehearsed, from his lips as if he'd been practicing it for a long time. "And she has to know what the score is before she can deal with it."

He reached for and held her hands reassuringly, using every bit of his professional training to keep on top of the situation. He did not allow himself to think of last night, or to see her as anything more than someone who needed his guidance and help. "There are a few things you need to know, about Liz and about me. We'll start with Liz."

He spoke as if to someone who couldn't understand the language very well. Angela was too grateful to be insulted, suddenly feeling as though she were in an alien world where her brain threatened to shut down with each passing word.

"Okay?" he asked, squeezing her hands. "Okay" he said at her nod. "As we've tried to make you see before, the reason that Liz is here in the first place is that her cancer didn't respond to the traditional treatments. Therefore, the doctors didn't hold out much hope for her. Now, while it's true that occasionally we do see cases of remission, we don't often, and in Liz's case we haven't so far. She's been getting a little worse each day, more so after we brought her back from the mountain."

"But the new medication," Angela said quickly, ready to grasp at any available straw. "Why would you give her a new medication if you'd already given up hope?"

"Because in previous experiments the results were promising, and because for a while, Benjy, who has the same kind of cancer that Liz does, seemed to rally under its use. And because Liz doesn't have anything to lose." He detailed every reason, wishing he didn't have to be the one to do so. "*Hope* is one thing, Angela. Expectation is another. That's why, just a few hours ago, Liz's doctor made the decision to call Janet and have her fly in to the States to be with her daughter. I was supposed to tell you, and I would have," he assured her quickly, "just as soon as I'd finished with this appointment."

"Why were they taking all the blood for tests?" Angela asked, then looked away, an icy fear hitting her chest at speeding-bullet velocity.

"Angel, look at me," he said gently. "I didn't rush right over to the cafeteria to tell you about Liz because I was trying to find a way to tell you at the same time that I'm not an invincible knight in shining armor. But there is no easy way." His voice cracked then, his emotions breaking through the carefully erected barriers he'd put up. "Angel, when I didn't want you to promise me forever last night, it wasn't because I didn't want to have a forever with you. It was because *I* couldn't promise *you* the same in return. Angel, I can't even guarantee you a year, let alone a forever. My cancer is in remission in that they think they got it all when they took my foot and the piece of my leg. As far as they can tell, I've been okay for a year now. But even if my blood tests prove as positive as everyone thinks they will, there aren't many people in the odds business who would bet good money on me for a while yet."

A cry from somewhere deep within her escaped her tightly constricted throat. And the agony inside of her was mirrored on his face, albeit for different reasons. She was in love with a man who might die! In love with a man who had good reason not to believe in Liz's recovery, in dreams for the future, or in miracles that hadn't happened when he'd needed them. How could she stand it if first Liz then he died? Her own personality would surely die with them. No one could take that much pain and still be an optimist. The doubts and the instinctive desire to flee what she couldn't fight took over her mind for a brief minute before the love she felt for him overcame and conquered the insecurity. She loved him, no matter what the future might hold for them. She had no intention of abandoning him now, as the first woman he thought had loved him had done. She loved him way too much for that.

But David hadn't waited to see her natural courage fight her fear of the dragon into submission. He'd seen the fear. He'd seen her natural desire to escape the horror that only *might be*. And he had assumed the worst.

"Don't say anything." He rejected the words her mind was even then trying to pair with her emotions and string together into a coherent reply. "I've heard it all before, and I don't need to hear it again. I know it's a shock, and I should have told you before we got involved. I just couldn't." He kissed her cheek softly, his lips clinging to her skin as if they wanted the contact to last longer than he did. "I wanted you too much. I wanted at least the fantasy, for one night, that it was going to last forever. I can't say that I'm proud of myself for taking advantage of you, but at least you can be comforted in knowing that I won't expect you to go through with any repeat performances. I had my one night. But that's over now and I don't expect you to pretend otherwise."

Angela's eyes grew wide as what he was saying sank in.

"In fact," he went on quickly, "it might be better all the way around if you left camp. It won't do you any good to stay and watch Liz grow weaker each day. I think, knowing you, that having to watch would destroy you."

Angela's mouth worked like a fish out of water and she turned an incredulous eye to Sylvia.

"You don't know how sorry I am that I can't produce a miracle for you." David shook his head. "You can't begin to know how sorry I am that I can't be your knight in shining armor. I hope that when this is all over you can find someone who is someday. You deserve to."

Releasing her hands, he didn't even look back as he walked out of the room and out of her life.

She stared, dumbfounded, at the space he'd just vacated.

Sylvia pursed her lips regretfully and put a comforting arm around Angela's shaking shoulders. David had been right all along. And there was nothing left to do but try to pick up the pieces for both of them. "I know how you must feel," Sylvia began.

"No! You don't!" Angela threw off Sylvia's hand in disgust, and directed her anger at David on the only other person present. "You don't if you think I must feel how he thinks I must feel. As if how I would feel was something *he*, unimaginative thing that he is, could predict. As if I were the same kind of shallow person as that ninny who let him walk out of her life. As though how and what I would feel was something he could pull out of a textbook!" She angrily paced the room. "I'm so mad I can't even begin to *tell* you how mad I feel." She picked up the paper gown and, shredding it in frustration, flung it to the floor like so much confetti.

"That man! That high-handed, overbearing, almost doctor know-it-all macho man needs to have his *head* examined a lot more than he needs a checkup on the rest of him. If he actually believes any of that garbage, he really must have gotten his psychology degree from a Cracker Jack box. And he must be missing more than his foot. He's got to be missing all the convoluted gray matter that's supposed to reside between his ears! The big numbskull!"

She ranted and raved in front of an astonished Sylvia, sharing only an intelligible word here and there.

"Thinks I'm so fragile I'm going to be destroyed, does he? Thinks he has the right to tell me when to go, does he? Thinks I care more about the quantity than the quality of life? Me? Ha! Shouldn't stay? Wild horses couldn't drag me away now. Thinks he's heard it all, does he? He hasn't heard anything yet!" She faced a shell-shocked Sylvia who was still struggling to understand. "Cowardly knight. Run out on me, will he? Sorry? Ha! He doesn't know the meaning of the word. Yet!"

A slow smile grew and spread the width of Sylvia's face. "I take it you're not going to leave him."

"Leave him? No," she fumed. "But if he's not careful, I'm going to tie his shoelaces together so he won't find it so easy to put either of his feet in his mouth." She tapped her fingers on the examining table. "Do you know if he's going to the costume party tonight?"

"I'm sure he's not." Sylvia shook her head. "He never has before."

"See to it that he does tonight," she ordered. "I don't care if you have to drown him in medicinal Scotch and pour him through the door. Just get him there for me and I'll do the rest."

"I'll find a way," Sylvia promised with a growing interest. "But what are you going to do?"

Angela ran down a growing mental list. "I'm going to make Liz's angel suit even if she can't wear it tonight. I'm going to steal David's leather jacket to give to a camp punk rocker. I'm going to try to find a costume for myself so I don't have to come as Lady Godiva. And last but not least, I'm going to devise a way to convince that hardheaded psychologist once and for all that I love him in the for-better-or-for-worse kind of way, until death do us part, however long that is."

Sylvia admired the determined woman. "David is a wonderful psychologist for other people. But like the plumber with the stopped-up sink, and the roofer with the leak over his bed, David tends to overlook his own problems. When they did the operation, David somehow began to see the possibility of a shortened life as the probability of a shortened life and he planned his remaining time around it. David knows how to die. What he needs now is someone who can teach him how to live. Do you think you can do that?"

"I can do anything," Angela said with renewed conviction. "I believe in making miracles come true."

"And if David won't come to the same conclusion?"

"He will," Angela promised. "He will or I'll take my rose-colored glasses off and shove my optimistic fist into his pessimistic nose!"

Eleven

There were times in the next four hours when Angela wondered if what she was attempting to pull off might not be under the heretofore empty heading of impossible.

Finding someone she knew in Los Angeles to find a movie studio willing to loan her a knight-in-shining-armor costume had been hard enough. Convincing them to rent it and then transport it the two hundred miles to the camp had used up every favor she possessed along with a goodly amount of her checking account. And once it was there, the fun had just begun. Calling on Sylvia to keep David otherwise occupied, she'd enlisted the aid of a conglomerate of conspiratorial campers to help her sneak the bulky metal suit into the cafeteria. From then on, there was no denying them access to the plot. She had their promise of silence only so long as they got to help. And of course, everyone had a friend who wanted in on the secret as well.

By the time eight o'clock rolled around, it seemed

as though everyone in camp, with the exception of David, not only knew about her plan but was intimately involved with pulling it off as well. The air was filled with a sense of barely controlled excitement, and every gnome, punk rocker, clown, and warty toad she'd danced with had grilled her on the details just to make sure they had it all right. Sylvia was going to bring David to the dance whenever she could. A lookout at the door was going to give them advance warning. Angela, in her damsel-in-distress costume, was then going to climb up on a low stage in the middle of the room where the knight stood, with an open, empty visor. After the children had produced the man to fill the costume, they were going to put him in it, one way or another, and keep him from escaping long enough for her to give him a handmade favor.

And then the men in the little white coats were going to come and take them away, ha-ha, to the funny farm, where life was beautiful all the time. . . . Angela pulled the white satin favor out of her conical, beribboned lady-in-distress hat, and read the words again. She'd stitched them quickly, after making Liz's angel costume, and so the embroidering was somewhat less than perfect, but still legible.

"Without you I can't banish the dragons, for no other knight could ever fill your shoes. Marry me?" She whispered the words to herself and glanced over at the waiting knight, who boasted a pair of familiar-looking orange tennis shoes. He was not going to understand this. He was going to kill her.

"He's coming! He's coming!" The chorus filled the room as the one lookout passed the news along to everyone else.

"I'm going. I'm going." Angela stood up to tell them all to forget it, only to find herself lifted up beside the tennis-shoe-shod knight.

"He's right outside!" Nick yelled from the door. "Kill the lights!"

As a dramatic touch, it had been decided, not by her, that when David first came in, it would be to a pitch-dark room. Somebody would lead him to center stage, as it were, and then hit the floodlights. She had a feeling this was all getting just a little bit out of hand.

"Are you ready?" a voice from out of the darkness asked her.

"No."

"Good." They weren't even listening to her. "We're going to bring him in now."

"David! David! David!" Angela's ears reverberated with the high-spirited chanting. It quieted down as the sound of someone approached. Angela frowned, trying to make out the sound. It wasn't footsteps quite. Step, clip, clop-clop, step, clip, clop-clop. Huh? She peered ahead in the darkness to try to see whatever was making the noise, but she couldn't see anything, her eyes still not attuned to the darkness after the earlier brightness of the room. How the children were doing it, heaven only knew.

"David?" Angela jumped as a familiar hand clasped hers, guided there by a host of helpers.

"It's me," an amused voice answered her from the darkness. "I don't know why you should be so surprised. You must have known that Sylvia would find a way to get me here. She spent the afternoon making sure I'd come."

"What did she say?" She squinted curiously, wishing she could see him.

"She said that you hadn't given up on me and that I shouldn't give up on you either. She said that you weren't like my ex-fiancée, that you were one dreamer who made her dreams come true with hard work and elbow grease. She said that you made your miracles happen by believing in them so hard that they *had* to come true. She told me that you were strong enough to wish for the impossible, and do everything in your power to make it possible, but that you wouldn't be devastated if it didn't live up to your expectations."

"She said all that?" The darkness began to give way to gray shadow in front of her eyes, showing her David's outline. What was he wearing? *What was he holding on to?*

"That and a lot more. Of course, she wasn't the only one to come and tell me what a complete ass I was being."

Several muffled giggles reached Angela's ears. Oh, they wouldn't have! They promised! The shadowy haze receded, giving her a gray and white look at what he was wearing. With a silky white long-sleeved shirt, left unbuttoned to the middle, a pair of tight black pants, red sash, and an eye patch, he made an absolutely dashing pirate. But it was the tinfoil-covered sword, and, most of all, the genuine wooden peg leg that drew her attention.

"Did anybody happen to mention that I love you? That I'll always love you?"

"I think fifty or sixty people *did* mention something to that effect this afternoon, right after they told me you'd gone out and imported a knight suit for me. Of course, that was after I'd rigged up a costume of my own. But that's fine. If they hadn't told me what you were doing, I might not have gotten the idea for your charger."

The house lights went up just as David pulled his charger forward with a familiar clop-clopping sound. Angela gasped in astonishment as one of the camp ponies trotted up, a glittery construction-paper horn taped between his ears.

"It's impossible, I know," David told her seriously. "Just like I thought your love for me was. But it's here, and so am I."

Angela's eyes filled with happy tears as she took the hat off and brought forth the satin favor. "You were supposed to be wearing the knight's costume when I gave you this, but I don't care what you wear as long as you say yes." She thrust it into his fingers and waited for him to read it and give her an answer. Patience had never been one of her virtues.

"I have something for you too." He unstrapped a package from the pony's back, previously hidden by a gaudy charger's trappings. "I went out and bought it before I was informed that you'd already gotten another costume."

"Open it! Open it! Open it! Open it!" their audience shouted, making Angela wonder who was on whose side here. She glanced at some of the excited painted faces. Did they know more than they were telling?

"I'm afraid I can't give you an answer until you change costumes." David crossed stubborn arms over his pirate's chest. "Wearing this costume is absolutely essential for what I have in mind."

Angela unwrapped the gift and watched in complete and utter astonishment as a real white satin-and-lace wedding gown tumbled forth and into her arms, the train spilling out all over the suit of armor and the children underneath. "My God," she whispered hoarsely. "This isn't a costume.

You bought this for me?" Before anyone else had talked to him?

"It was a risk I had to take," he told her forthrightly. "I couldn't let you go. I tried, but I just couldn't. I had to try to win your love. And it *is* a costume. It's the only costume I've dreamed of seeing you in since the day we met."

Pirate and lady met somewhere between the suit of armor and the unicorn, the wedding dress spread out like a promise.

"Will you marry me?" he asked her breathlessly. "I know I'm not the perfect knight, but—"

"But without you I can't banish the dragons." She quoted from the favor. "Because no one else can fill your shoes." She kissed him with delighted abandon to a background of wild cheering. "Yes, I'll marry you, now, tomorrow, whenever you say."

"I don't know if Liz is going to be able to act as our flower girl by then, but we could hop on our unicorn charger and head over to the hospital to ask."

"What?" Her eyes flew to his, silently begging him not to tease her.

"I got a call from Benjy's doctor late this afternoon to say that while Benjy was still very, very weak, he had come out of the coma. When I got off the telephone, Liz's doctor came in to say that he didn't think it would be necessary to have Janet fly in after all. The medication works slowly, but if it has the chance to work, it eventually brings about an improvement in many cases." He smiled broadly. "I thought you might want Janet to fly over anyway to be your matron of honor."

The waiting crowd clapped and Angela cried out in exuberant relief, the miracles coming almost too fast to count.

"I'm not the perfect knight," he felt compelled to remind her one last time. "I still don't know if I can promise you a forever."

She swirled the wedding dress veil over both their heads, securing for them the only privacy to be found in the place. She kissed him soundly, vowing to find somewhere a little less silly-looking to finish her explanation. "I never asked you for forever. All I wanted was a happily forever after. Think you can manage that?"

"That." He nodded with a loving, intimate smile. "That, and a lot more."

THE EDITOR'S CORNER

Thanks for all your wonderful cards and letters telling us how glad you are that we've added two LOVESWEPTS to our monthly publishing list. Obviously, it's quite a lot of additional work, and, so, we are especially glad to welcome Kate Hartson as our new senior editor. Kate has been in publishing for more than seven years and has edited many different kinds of works, but in the last few years she has devoted a great deal of her time to romance fiction and has edited almost one hundred love stories. Kate is as fine a person as she is an editor, and we are delighted to have her on our team.

You have six delicious treats to anticipate next month from Peggy Webb, Sandra Brown, Joan Elliott Pickart, Kay Hooper, Charlotte Hughes, and Iris Johansen. I probably don't need to say more than those six names to make you eager to get at the books—but I had so much fun working on them that it would be virtually impossible for me to restrain myself from sharing my enthusiasm with you.

Peggy Webb presents a heartrending love story in **PRIVATE LIVES,** LOVESWEPT #216. John Riley is a man whose brilliant singing career has left him somewhat burned out; Sam Jones is an enchanting woman who blunders into his rural retreat and brings more sunshine and fresh tickling breezes into his life than he could get in the great outdoors. This moving romance is a bit of a departure into more serious emotional writing for Peggy, though she doesn't leave her characteristic humor behind. Her lovers are wonderful, and we think their healing power on each other will leave you feeling marvelous long after you've finished reading about their **PRIVATE LIVES.**

FANTA C, Sandra Brown's LOVESWEPT #217, is a sheer delight. On the surface heroine Elizabeth Burke seems to be a bit straitlaced, but her occupation—and her daydreams—reveal her to be a sensual and romantic lady. She owns and operates a boutique in a large hotel called Fantasy, where she sells such items as silk lingerie and seductive perfumes. It is in her rich and powerful fantasy life that she expresses her real self . . . until neighbor Thad Randolph comes to her rescue, dares to fulfill her secret dreams, and turns fantasy into reality. A keeper, if there ever was one!

LUCKY PENNY by Joan Elliott Pickart is LOVESWEPT #218 and another real winner from this talented and prolific author. Penelope Chapman is a complicated woman with a wealth of passion and sweet sympathy beneath her successful exterior. Cabe Malone is a man who secretly yearns for a woman to cherish and build a life with. They meet when Cabe finds her weeping in the house he is building . . . and his very protective instinct is aroused. Soon, though, Penny must flee, and Cabe sets off in hot pursuit. A breathlessly exciting chase ensues, and you'll cheer when these two lovable people capture each other.

News Flash! Kay Hooper is being held hostage by a band of

(continued)

dangerous, sexy men, and they aren't going to let her go until she's finished telling the love story of each and every one of them. And aren't we lucky? Fasten your seatbelts, because with **RAFFERTY'S WIFE**, LOVESWEPT #219, Kay is going to sweep you away on another glorious caper. This time that sneaky Hagen has Rafferty Lewis and Sarah Cavell in his clutches. He's assigned them the roles of husband and wife on an undercover assignment that takes them to an island paradise in the midst of revolution. But Rafferty and Sarah are falling deeply, hopelessly in love, and their madness for each other is almost as desperate as the job they have to do. Watch out for Sereno . . . and don't think that just because Raven and Josh are on their honeymoon they are going to be out of the romantic action. It's only fair to tell you that Kay has created a marvelous series for you. Look next for **ZACH's LAW**, then **THE FALL OF LUCAS KENDRICK,** then . . . well, more on this from me next month!

Exciting, evocative, and *really original* aptly describe, LOVESWEPT #220, **STRAIGHT SHOOTIN' LADY** by Charlotte Hughes. When Maribeth Bradford comes to the bank in her small town to interview with its handsome new president for a job, she walks into a robbery in progress. Suddenly, she finds herself bound back-to-back with devastatingly attractive Edward Spears and locked with him in a dark closet. . . . And that's just the beginning of a great love story between a devoted small-town gal and a city slicker with a lot of adjustments to make. We think you're going to be utterly charmed by this wonderful romance.

THE SPELLBINDER, LOVESWEPT #221, by Iris Johansen delivers precisely what the title promises—a true spellbinder of a love story. Brody Devlin can hypnotize an audience as easily as he can overwhelm a woman with his virile good looks. Sacha Lorion is a waif with wild gypsy beauty who has a claim on Brody. Her past is dark, mysterious, dangerous . . . and when her life is threatened, Brody vows to protect her. Both of them swiftly learn that they must belong to one another body and soul . . . 'til death do them part. This is a magnificent story full of force and fire.

Enjoy!

Sincerely,

Carolyn Nichols

Carolyn Nichols
    Editor

LOVESWEPT
Bantam Books, Inc.
666 Fifth Avenue
New York, NY 10103

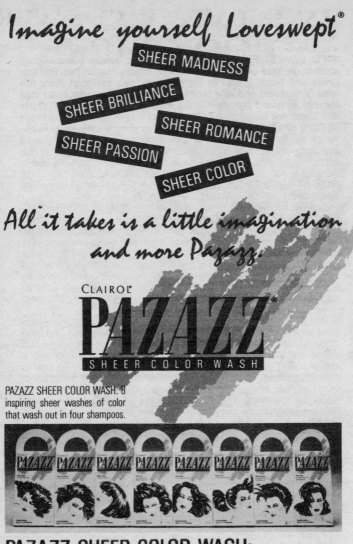

HANDSOME, SPACE-SAVER
BOOKRACK